Whispers of Hope

Whispers of Hope

A NOVEL

MARCIE ANNE JENSON

Covenant Communications, Inc.

Cover design copyrighted 2000 by Covenant Communications, Inc.

Published by Covenant Communications, Inc.
American Fork, Utah

Printed in the United States of America
First Printing: August 2000

07 06 05 04 03 02 01 00   10 9 8 7 6 5 4 3 2 1

ISBN 1-57734-707-2

Library of Congress Cataloging-in-Publication Data

Jenson, Marcie Ann, 1959-
    Whispers of hope / Marcie Anne Jenson.
      p. cm.
    ISBN 1-57734-707-2
    1. Intercountry adoption—Fiction. 2. Chilean Americans—Fiction. 3. Children—Death—Fiction.
    4. Adopted children—Fiction. 5. Orphans—Fiction. I. Title.
    PS3560.E597 W48 2000
    813'.6--dc21   00-043048
                                   CIP

To my children whose lives fill me with hope

ACKNOWLEDGMENTS:

Thank you to Mom and Dad, Sandy and Kerri. Your encouragement lent me the courage to complete this story. Much appreciation to Shauna Nelson, the most wonderful of editors, and to the insightful staff at Covenant for making this dream a reality.

PROLOGUE

After calling 911, Ty Edwards left his car. Struggling against the wind, he stumbled down the cliffs, toward a small cove of pebbly sand, toward the incoming tide, toward his buddy who was somewhere in those waves. "THES!" he screamed at the churning sea. "THESEUS LAUTARO FLETCHER! THES!" A thought blew in his mind like a grenade. Theseus Lautaro Fletcher. His buddy's was a strange name for a newsflash, a headline, a tombstone.

Ty ran into the surf; the frigid water tugged at his tennis shoes, his socks, his jeans. He pictured Thes in his mind, the black hair and dark eyes. Ty swore at the ocean. He made bargains with God.

Ty knew Thes was a fighter. He was out there somewhere. Perhaps the ocean would throw Thes into his arms. Ty would drag his buddy out of the water to safety. He would pound his chest, and breathe into his blue lips, and life would return to those black, dark-lashed eyes. Ty prayed for a miracle. But no miracle came. The young man sobbed as he stared at the sea.

Then the image of Thes's younger sister, Dennie, rose in his mind. He saw the accusing glare she had thrown at him when she noticed the beer in the car before he and Thes left that morning.

Unbidden, his mind turned to a hot September day sixteen months ago, the day Dennie turned sixteen. After football practice, he remembered going home with Thes for a dip in the pool. Dennie had been swimming laps, her compact body cutting smoothly through the water, her long, black hair streaming behind her.

She had stopped and pulled herself onto the side, her feet dangling in the blue. Ty and Thes dove off the board. Like an olympic judge, Dennie put up eight fingers for Thes's flip. Nine fingers for Ty's back dive. She had giggled as they argued about the scores.

"Den, watch out for Ty," Thes had said when he leapt from the pool and ran into the house to catch a phone call.

"What?" Ty remembered gesturing innocently, his wrists bending, and his hands in the air. Then Ty had swum to where Dennie sat. He had teased her about turning sixteen, about her strict Mormon parents, her protective brother. "Sweet sixteen and never been kissed." He had laughed and tugged on her toes.

Dennie had jumped into the water and splashed him. He had grabbed her hands. Then he had kissed her. Afterwards, her eyes had looked confused, but soft and beautiful, as if saying, *But this is my brother's best friend. But this is Ty.* He had felt a tremendous urge to hold her. Then, the slider door had opened and Dennie had jumped away. Thes had leapt into the pool, creating a splash that nearly drowned them both.

A gull screeched overhead pulling Ty back into the present. "NO!" Ty's voice disappeared in the wind. He ducked his head and pounded his body forward, deeper into the waves. A wave covered him. Water blinded and numbed him. Then, strangers' arms were around him, gathering him to the shore.

Back on the coarse sand, away from the waves, he realized that the strange choking sounds were coming from himself. A uniformed man with a drenched mustache, who was an inch shorter than Ty and half Ty's breadth, locked his arms around Ty and held him until he could breathe again.

When Ty's breath came more evenly, he focused on the uniformed men, the ambulance, and the police cars. Ty heard their questions and, swallowing, he told them the lie: that his buddy, Thes Fletcher, had drowned because he was trying to save the life of his best friend who had fallen off the rocks while fishing. "He died for me. He died trying to save me," Ty said. Then, he hung his head, half wishing he were in the water with his best friend, Theseus Lautaro Fletcher. At peace.

CHAPTER 1

Black Clouds in a Turquoise Sky

Dennie Fletcher, seventeen years old and a junior in high school, looked out the window at California's deep-turquoise sky. The clouds hung black, and the sliver of moon shone like an arch cut from the sky. Dennie shivered and pulled her blue-green sweatshirt on over her black jeans. She lifted her black hair from the nape of the sweatshirt and shook it out. Her hair sloped past her shoulders, shiny and soft like a piece of ebony silk. She ran her fingers through it and felt its heaviness as it hung to her waist. She heard the lonely cry of a train whistle. The sound of the locomotive moving into the distance was like an echo of her sorrow.

Dennie sat down on the couch and reached for a photo album on the coffee table. It was brown leather with the raised gold letters *In Celebration of Your Life* printed on the front. For a moment, her fingers caressed the letters. Everything—the sky, the photo album, the very air she breathed—reminded her of her brother, of the fact that he was gone forever, and of her relentless feeling of guilt, the whisper that she could have prevented his death.

Dennie opened the photo album. The first picture was taken twelve years ago on the day that Dennie and Thes, two orphans from Chile, had flown to the United States to meet their new parents. They were just two little kids, between the ages of five and seven, standing in an airport, holding a sign that said *Welcome Home*. In the photo, Dennie looked like she had just awakened. A dorky pink bow hung crookedly in her hair. But Thes's eyes shone bright like shiny black stones as if he were devising a way to steal all of the Cinnabons in the airport. Mounted below the picture, there was a poem written by Meryl Fletcher, Dennie and Thes's adoptive mother.

> *You*
> *Thes Lautaro Fletcher*
> *Came to us with Denizen*
> *On airplane wings like magic*
> *Dark-eyed orphan from Chile*
> *With sun and storm in your gaze*
> *Did you come that I might heal you?*
> *Or did you heal*
> *Me?*

Dennie heard a knock. She shut the album and flipped off the lamp before opening the front door.

"O-lee-o," Aimy Tomlinson, Dennie's best friend and across-the-street neighbor, sliced into the darkening entryway. Aimy wove her fingers through her bangs, pushing her short, white-blonde hair back from her eyes. "Density, you need to turn some lights on. It's evening, in case you didn't notice." Aimy turned on the hall switch, and the artificial light made her pixie face appear even paler against the spattering of freckles. Her leather jacket hung over her arm, and the neon words on her black T-shirt read: *DON'T INTERPRET THIS SMILE AS HAPPINESS, IT'S INSANITY.*

"In my family we turn off the lights when we leave. Saves electricity," Dennie said as she turned to flip the lights off again.

"Beware of intensity, Density," Aimy laughed. Before hitting the switch, Dennie caught her own image in the hallway mirror. Her eyes were wide set and so dark that the pupils were barely visible. The lids behind them were light and arched. Her cheeks were deep auburn, thanks to Cover Girl® blush, her nose was larger and more prominent than she liked, and her lips were moist and full. Then, Dennie wondered the same thing she had wondered countless times over the past four weeks. *How could she look the same when her brother, Thes, was dead? How could she continue to exist now that the world was a tilting place, disjointed and obscure with dark holes that people could fall into at any moment?*

Twenty minutes later, Aimy and Dennie arrived at the Grantlin drag strip. They made their way to the bleachers where they spotted

Blake Taylor, Dennie's uncle, sitting with his date, Karin Parker. Karin was in her early thirties and had moved to Grantlin three years ago. Blake and Karin stood up and enthusiastically swung their arms above their heads as if Aimy and Dennie were shipwrecked sailors whom they were motioning aboard to rescue.

Aimy crinkled her upturned nose as the girls mounted the bleachers. "Adults can be such dorks. I wish Sister Parker wasn't here. She drives me crazy. Her hair is *so* orange."

"They've been dating a lot lately," Dennie remarked as they neared a group of shirtless guys with their upper bodies painted green. The boys whistled and the air was rank with the sweetish stench of marijuana.

"We've got room," one of the guys invited.

"Sure thing!" Aimy grinned and acted like she was about to take a seat.

"She's kidding." Dennie grabbed Aimy's arm and steered her around the boys to the place where Blake and Karin were sitting.

"Hi." Blake Taylor squeezed Dennie's hand and kissed her cheek. Karin reached an arm around Aimy's angular shoulder. Aimy shook off the arm and dropped onto the bleacher in front of Blake.

Blake Taylor watched as Dennie sat down next to Aimy. His thoughts turned to both of the girls. How sharp and thin Aimy looked tonight! It had been two weeks since she had attended his seminary class. He hadn't seen her at church either. Blake hoped it wasn't because she was involved with Brak Meyers once more. Blake remembered a time, months ago, when Aimy had brought Brak to church. He was a handsome boy, tall with charcoal-black hair and alabaster skin. But he kept himself aloof and coldly sluffed aside the missionaries' smiling overtures. Thes and Dennie's behavior towards Brak that Sunday bordered on rudeness. They hardly spoke to him. When Blake had asked them why, they had whispered that they hated the way he treated Aimy, and they were livid with Aimy for allowing it. But that was in the past.

Blake's thoughts turned to Dennie, his niece. By nature she was soft-spoken, intelligent and caring. Yet, since Thes's death she had become so quiet, so inward. It was as if her soul was folded away somewhere, deep inside. This worried him. Blake pushed his hand into his coat pocket and felt the journal he had purchased for her. He hoped it would help.

Blake's thoughts moved backwards in time to Thes's funeral. He had wanted to remain composed for Dennie, and for Meryl and Rick, his sister and brother-in-law. But instead he had sobbed, his eyes swollen like the ocean that had taken his nephew's life. And the emotion that had racked his body was not only for the loss of Thes but also for the stoic, silent way in which Dennie bore her grief—as if she were alone in the universe, with pain too terrible to permit her to weep.

"You both look *so* cute tonight," Karin's friendly voice scattered Blake's thoughts while it scratched like fingernails on Aimy's chalkboard nerves. "I was *so* excited when Blake told me you were coming," Karin went on. "I love your shoes, Dennie. Aimy, with your jacket unzipped, you remind me of my little Christopher. He doesn't seem to feel the cold! That T-shirt is a riot! Where did you get it?"

"The Gemini store," Aimy said shortly. Karin's chatter was driving her insane! Couldn't the woman just quit talking?

"That's such a unique place," Karin continued, unaware of Aimy's irritation. "Your mom does hair there, doesn't she? I walked by the store a few days ago and saw some cute things in the store window. I almost went in. I like how they do massages and hair. They have so many unique knickknacks. But then I thought about how they have a psychic there, telling fortunes. I decided not to go in. I don't think I would even *want* to know the future. Not only because we're Mormons and that kind of thing is taboo. It would be too scary. My everyday life teaching kindergarten and raising Chris is scary enough. Aimy, I admire your mom for her ability to raise you alone. What are her secrets?"

"Gemstone pendants." Aimy said, making her tone smooth and harmless as butter.

"Gemstone pendants?" Karin questioned. "What would gemstone pendants have to do with raising a child?"

"You know, gemstones—they have certain almost magical properties." Now Aimy became the knife cutting into the butter. "You should try them. Chrysocolla increases feminine qualities like communication and creativity. Not that you aren't feminine of course. But it might help you with communication—knowing when to talk and when to be quiet."

Karin's color heightened and her mouth formed a small *O*, like she wanted to say something but wasn't sure what it was. Aimy went on, "Then there's Tourmaline for the weak-hearted. It alleviates fear. Double-terminated clear quartz crystal gives energizing clarity. So you can make better choices. It might help you consider a different color for your hair, something less brassy. My mom could help you at the Gemini Store."

Dennie noticed Blake's arm tighten around Karin. Aimy's rudeness was getting to him. But Dennie knew her uncle. She knew he would be patient, that he wouldn't make a scene.

Karin took a breath and chose to let Aimy's hurtful comments slip from her, much like water sliding off a duck's back. Her cheerful voice shredded the uncomfortable silence. "Couldn't we all use energizing clarity? And look! The race is about to begin!"

A moment later the jet cars began to race. The horizon, formerly as black as Dennie's eyes, was dimmed by fire and smoke. Blake explained that the cars with the slowest dial times got a head start. A dial time was like a golf handicap.

"So the fastest cars give the slower cars a break. That's really nice," Karin grinned.

Dennie sat back down and gazed at the strange cars with their round, fat, back tires and their fronts like little vacuums. She saw the white smoke, the fire and light as they sped down the tracks. She heard the roar of the engines, smelled the rubber burning, watched the bright safety parachutes flare open, slowing the speeding cars. She heard the crowd cheer.

But as Dennie watched, she shuddered. The chill air on her cheeks felt as cold as Thes's baby finger the day she slipped the CTR ring on before they lowered the lid of his coffin.

Later that night, Dennie sat on the worn chocolate-brown couch in the den leafing through a novel she was supposed to have read for her Honors English class. Lately, she couldn't concentrate. She'd never get through the book. Luckily, she had checked out the explanatory notes from the library. She'd rely on them for tomorrow's test. Her English teacher, Ms. Harris, would probably notice, but she couldn't help that. She heard the front door open and footsteps in the hall. Stiffening, she half expected her dead brother to enter the room.

"Hey, Denz, it's me." Dennie recognized Uncle Blake's voice as he sauntered into the room. "You guys ought to lock the front door."

"I forgot." Dennie relaxed a bit and tucked her feet beneath her. Blake stretched out in the desk chair and crossed his ankles. "I thought you'd be asleep by now. But after I dropped Karin off, I drove by and saw the light on. You've always been a den rat. Where's your mom and dad?"

"Asleep," Dennie answered.

"Figures. It's almost midnight, kid. If you don't hit the hay, you'll turn into a pumpkin. You'll be too tired for seminary in the morning. Don't forget it's *Donut Friday*."

"Not that you'd let me forget," Dennie answered with a slow smile. "What about you, Uncle Blake-o? What do we do if the teacher dozes?"

"I'm bringing my guitar. I composed a song about Moses and we're going to make beautiful music!"

"Good luck," Dennie said. She didn't ask to hear the song, to sing it with him. She always used to, but she didn't have the energy tonight.

"What do you *thing*," Blake's tired voice slurred, then straightened. "I mean *think* about Karin and me?"

"I *thing* you're tired and I *think* she's nice," Dennie teased as she looked up at her uncle.

"I want to get to know her better. I'm almost forty. That's over the hill, beyond the beyond. I might marry her."

"Because you're *beyond the beyond?*" Dennie queried.

"Because I'm falling in love with her," Uncle Blake answered, shrugging helplessly. He stood up and reached into the big pocket of his coat. "I have something for you." He handed Dennie a journal with an impressionistic picture of the ocean and sky on the front.

"Thanks," Dennie said hesitantly as she fingered the blank pages. "What's it for?"

"To write in."

"I know that. I mean it's not my birthday or anything. What's the occasion? You could have given me a computer disk to write on."

Uncle Blake looked at the ceiling, then back at Dennie. "There's this writer named Camus who said something about how we can't escape the common lot of pain. If our pain is justified it's only if we speak on behalf of those who can't tell their own story. I can't speak for Thes. Your mom and dad can't either. We weren't there the first six or seven years of his life. It's up to you."

"I can't do it," Dennie muttered. "I wasn't there when he died. Ty Edwards was. Maybe you should give this to him." Thoughts pounded in her head. *Uncle Blake, I can't do it because I know too much, I hid too much! Then Ty lied about how Thes died. Now it's too late. Too late for the truth.*

"You don't have to write anything. Just keep it in case you change your mind." Uncle Blake patted Dennie's shoulder. "I love ya, kid. See ya in the morning." Blake Taylor left.

The journal felt heavy in Dennie's hands. When she stood up she found she was shaking. As Dennie clutched the journal to her heart she found herself wishing it would disappear.

Later that night, as Dennie lay sleeplessly in bed, she felt the journal's presence in her room. *OK, Uncle Blake, I'll write it,* she thought. *But afterwards I'll hide it. I won't let anyone read it. Not Mom and Dad, or even you, Uncle Blake, you who found Thes and me and brought us here. The truth would hurt too much. The rumors must die like the wind. That guy, Camus, said that pain is justified when we write for someone who can't tell their own story. Does that justify guilt as well? And what if no one ever reads the story? But, I'll write it. For Lautaro. And Mina.*

CHAPTER 2

A Hole in the Sky

Tonight, my Uncle Blake gave me this journal. Since I can't sleep, I'll write. I'll return to the past, before I came to America. Before I knew my mom, my dad, my Uncle Blake—before I was Dennie. It was so long ago. It is hard to know where memory stops and imagination begins.

I remember mountains, my toothless mama laughing in a hut with walls of thin wood, or were the walls of thick cardboard? I don't know anymore. I had a black-eyed brother, Lautaro. I was called Mina. I looked up the name in my Spanish-English Dictionary. Mina refers to a mine deep in the earth, but it can also mean source of fortune. What a strange name for a ragged five-year-old with dirty hands and filthy hair!

I remember rain. We were trapped in a cardboard room ringing with the woman's cough. Claws of hunger scraped my inside. I cried and Lautaro yelled for something to eat. The woman shouted for us to be still. She would go and bring back food. The flap of door opened and closed. She coughed in the rain. She had left us before . . .

The next day passed. She was still gone. Night came. A neighbor man gave us bread. "Your mother is dead," he said angrily. "Gather your things. My wife will come for you soon."

The man left. Lautaro jerked me to my feet, shouting that the man and his wife were bad. We had to leave. His hand gripped mine like iron as he took me into the night. First we walked as silent as shadows. A drunken man pointed at us and laughed, "You little ones think no one sees you? God can see you. The devil can see you. You little ones think you can escape? Ha!" Then, we ran. The rain stopped. There was a hole in the sky, a break in the clouds where a star shone through. I fell. Lautaro pulled me up. I cried and he told me to be strong. "Look at the star,

Mina. We must run to the star. Then we will be safe." But no matter how fast we ran, the star was always above and beyond.

We followed the star past the city lights. We slept under a bridge and the rain returned. In the morning, Lautaro trailed the dogs to the garbage and brought me food. Before he left he ordered me to be still. If no one knew we were here, then we would be safe. Lautaro came back with food. The hunger left, but not the fear. Then, Lautaro painted his face with mud and made me laugh. During the afternoon, Lautaro raced against the clouds, but could never catch up to them. At night, he huddled me to him, sharing his warmth against the ghost wind and the drumming rain. The Andes were the walls around us, the sky our roof. We lived that way for a day, maybe a week, maybe longer.

The music from Dennie's alarm smashed into her consciousness. She forced her eyes open. Seminary! NO! Her hand groped for the clock and shut off the noise. She couldn't get up! A terrible heaviness pushed her eyes closed, her body deeper under the covers. Then, a memory from the night before flitted through her. Uncle Blake was expecting her. Something about donuts and a song he had written. She had never been able to disappoint him. She opened the blinds. Black rain drummed through the darkness. Dennie forced herself out of bed and trusted the shower to erase the exhaustion.

Fifteen minutes later, Dennie plodded into the kitchen. The shower hadn't worked. She couldn't beat the tiredness. Her mom stood at the counter making fresh orange juice, adding a lone grapefruit before pouring Dennie a glass.

"Dennie, we didn't get a chance to talk much yesterday. I was so tired." Meryl Fletcher smiled at her daughter. She wore men's navy pajamas and her wheat-colored hair was wild from the night. "Did you have fun at the races? Ages ago I used to watch Blake race. It was great."

"It was fun." Dennie shouldered her backpack with one arm and simultaneously took a drink of juice using the other hand.

Her father, Rick Fletcher watched her as he entered the room. "Morning, Den. It takes talent to do two things at once. Don't spill the juice!" He wore a dark, tailored suit and a tie from Macy's. His receding hair was short and combed back. With his shoes on he was the same height as Dennie's mother. He poured some Cinnamon Crisp cereal.

"Morning, Dad," Dennie sampled her juice. For some reason it didn't taste as good as usual. Maybe it was the grapefruit.

"It's the grapefruit!" her father announced as if he had read Dennie's mind. "Meryl, tomorrow make the juice without the grapefruit. It's better without the grapefruit."

"Rick, the grapefruit adds depth. Your cereal's too sweet. It ruins the juice."

"Your mother should listen to me, don't you think?" Rick raised his eyebrows at Dennie.

"Your father shouldn't tell me what to do, don't you think?" Meryl replied, smiling.

"I'd better go," Dennie interrupted her parents.

"Dennie," her mother cajoled. "You should eat something solid before you go. Breakfast is the most important meal of the day. Did you know that people who eat breakfast live approximately five years longer than people who don't?"

"I'll live dangerously."

Her mother hugged her and sighed in parental defeat.

"Have a good day, Den," her father added. "Make sure you don't park too close to anyone else. We wouldn't want a ding in the Tahoe."

Dennie wanted to tell them that she was tired, tired to death of the same conversations every morning, the life-goes-on theme, the pretended cheerfulness. For a moment her hand shook and her juice nearly spilled. How would they feel if she told them the truth? Would they stand straight against its pounding horror? Would she see forgiveness in their eyes?

But they might crumble. She couldn't live if they crumbled. She had heard her mother cry at night. She had noticed the lines of grief around her father's eyes. But they still talked, and ate, and worked, and slept. Sometimes they even laughed. They kept going because they were proud of Thes. They believed he had died trying to save Ty's life. It justified their pain. It justified their terrible loss. She kept quiet. She could pretend too.

Moments later, Dennie pulled the car from the garage and backed up, straight across the street and, taillights first, into Aimy's driveway.

The world had changed from black to an inky, dripping gray. It was too early to honk the horn. Dennie yanked her hood over her head and ran to Aimy's door. She rang the doorbell and pounded hard. She waited and pounded again. Rain saturated her hood. She shivered. Aimy opened the door and yawned, clad in a long T-shirt. Her slim, freckled legs stuck out below it. To the left, a dusty fisherman's net hung in the corner of the front room with a lone dried starfish stuck in it. The house was cluttered and smelled musty.

"Density, I didn't get up on time. Sorry."

"You *told* me to pick you up this morning. Get dressed. I'll wait!"

"A bit testy today, aren't we? Come in, it's freezing!" Aimy pulled Dennie into the house and closed the door behind them.

"Is Moni still asleep?" Dennie asked as Aimy sloshed toothpaste down the sink. Aimy nodded and tucked the T-shirt she had worn all night into a short black skirt. She pulled black nylons over her legs, hiding the freckles. Her mother, Moni, had taught her how to dress, how to look cute and sexy—like Meg Ryan. But it was Aimy's job to keep things together, to cook and to clean, to make sure Moni got to work on time and that the bills were paid. Now that Thes was gone, only Dennie knew of Moni's depression, of her terrible headaches, of the pills she took to keep going. Only Dennie knew that Aimy spent many nights sleeping on the floor next to her mother's bed to make sure that her mother woke up in the mornings.

"I'll call her from seminary," Aimy said. "She should be up by then."

Aimy crunched mousse into her wet, yellow hair and pushed it back. "I'm ready. Let's hope Brother Blake-o doesn't faint when he sees me."

Ten minutes later the girls slipped into the back of their seminary class. Blake swept his arm in welcome and gestured toward a box of donuts as he continued his lecture. They each grabbed one and found seats.

"Try to imagine what it must have been like for Moses," Blake explained. "How alone he must have felt! Here he was a prince of Egypt, yet his people were slaves. He killed trying to protect one of his own. Instead of thanks he received derision and scorn. Moses was slow of speech, torn between two peoples. He knew discouragement. He knew fear. He knew doubt. But he became one of the mightiest prophets. He was a hero. He saved an entire nation and yet never was able to enter the Promised Land. I thought about all these things as I wrote this song about Moses. It's called *Alone in the Wilderness.*"

Ron Babcock, the bishop's son, grabbed Blake's guitar and handed it to him. "Ronny-boy is annoyingly helpful," Aimy whispered as she bit into a glazed donut.

Blake's long, blunt fingers flawlessly shifted from chord to chord as his gentle tenor voice filled the room:

A babe in a basket so hungry he weeps;
A princess now draws him near. When will he sleep?
Oh, God of Israel, bring him home.
In Egypt this child is alone.

The questions, the burning, the blood and the lie,
Alone in the wilderness, when will he die?
Oh, God of Israel, hear his cry,
"A prince or a slave? Who am I?"
A stranger in Midian, he stutters and turns,
The bush and the bright flame—It lives as it burns.
The God of Israel answers his plea,
"I am. I will set Israel free."

A life full of choices, the weight he must bear;
He looks at the Promised Land, but can't go there.
The God of Israel takes him home.
The child is no longer alone.

As sunset and darkness begin a new day,
Alone in the wilderness, we kneel to pray.
"God of Israel, grant that we
Too may be holy, like thee."

"Dennie, sing it with me a second time?" Blake asked. He passed out copies of the lyrics and added, "The third time, everybody join in."

For an instant, Dennie balked inwardly, feeling embarrassed and unsure. It was a haunting, Hebrew melody. The words were sad and beautiful. Blake winked at her. There was something lonely and entreating in his eyes. She decided to sing with her Uncle Blake. When she was small, he taught her to sing away the nightmares.

"Talent just runs in your family," Aimy quipped before they began. As they sang, the melody rang true. When the other students joined in, their voices were like shadows compared to the strength and life of the music coming from Dennie Fletcher and Blake Taylor. When the song ended, Ron Babcock clapped and whistled.

In the locker room, Dennie and Aimy changed into their red and gold PE clothes for sixth period. Once they were in the gym, they spotted Ron Babcock who was already dressed and was milling around the far court. Aimy waved to him. He started towards them using his bounce-walk gait. The girl's grinned at each other, then looked back at Ron, as the spring in Ron's step propelled him up and forward as he walked. Aimy headed toward Ron, imitating his bounce. With each step, she sprung up on her toe, almost a skip, then down again.

"Stop!" Ron yelled when he recognized what she was doing. He walked up to them stiff-legged. "I don't do that."

"You do," Dennie said as she joined them using the Ron Babcock walk.

Aimy laughed at her. "You're too short, Density. Ronny-boy, it's even worse when you run track! Spring! Spring! Spring!"

Ron's grin at the girls was wide and bright. Then Terrance Jamison, the principal, entered the gym, decked out in a stiff suit. Dennie noticed that Ron's grin evaporated and his mouth turned into a hard line. No one liked Jamison, but Ron's reaction still seemed extreme.

Jamison spoke, "Your teachers are attending a workshop today. I'll take you into the weight room where we'll join Mr. Bryon's class."

"Can I go outside and jog around the track?" Ron Babcock asked. The uncharacteristic coldness in his voice surprised Dennie. Ron, who was one of the best distance runners in the school, was usually Mr. Positive. But there were rumors that Mr. Jamison didn't like Ron's dad, a science teacher. Maybe that had something to do with Ron's tension.

"Babcock, if you're foolish enough to run in this weather, get out of here," Jamison barked.

Aimy and Dennie headed towards the weight room. "I wonder why Ronny-boy wants to run in the rain," Aimy mused. "Did you see the way he stared at Jamison, like he hated him or something? Not typical Ronny-boy."

When the girls entered the weight room, Brak Meyers sauntered up to them. Dennie took a deep breath. She couldn't stand the sight of him. His presence surprised her. He must have been transferred into Mr. Bryon's weight-training class this semester.

"Aimy, I'm going to be your personal trainer," Brak said as he caught Aimy's arm.

Aimy pulled her arm away. She had broken up with Brak right after Thes died. "In your dreams," she retorted. It bothered Dennie the way her supposedly angry tone rang like a tease.

"For old times sake," Brak smiled and put his arm around Aimy tightly. "Dennie, you come too. Let bygones be bygones."

Dennie shook her head. "Aimy, let's go," she began.

"I'm going to let Brak show me around," Aimy smiled sheepishly at Dennie. "Sure you don't want to join us?"

"Positive," Dennie said. What was Aimy doing? How could she give that jerk the time of day? Dennie whirled around and left the weight room.

"Miss Fletcher, where do you think you are going?" She heard Jamison's voice behind her.

"Outside. Jogging. Like Ron Babcock." Dennie fled into the locker room without waiting for a reply.

But she couldn't stay there. Jamison would check. She grabbed her jacket and ran outside. She found Ron Babcock moving swiftly around the track, gracefully bouncing through the drizzle. Dennie began jogging, sloshing steadily, consistently forward. Ron caught up with her and slowed down.

"Dennie Fletcher," he said cheerfully, sounding like his old self. "Wonderful weather we're having."

"Beautiful weather," Dennie answered sarcastically. They jogged together until Dennie's lungs burned and her breath turned ragged. She didn't have enough wind. "Go on ahead," she gasped to Ron. "I don't want to ruin your workout."

"You couldn't ruin my workout if you tried." Ron grinned cheerfully. He slowed to a walk so that Dennie could catch her breath. Then, he added teasingly, "Besides, I'd rather concentrate on *you* than Jamison."

"Why? What did Jamison do?" Dennie was still breathing hard. "I mean besides the fact that the man is tactless and charmless."

"The list is long. One example—last year some parents blamed my dad because their kids blew the AP Biology exam. These parents took their complaint to the school board. Jamison didn't support Dad. He made the school board question Dad's qualifications. He's done all he can to make Dad's life miserable ever since a funding controversy a couple of years ago."

Dennie nodded thoughtfully. Jamison was one of those people it wouldn't pay to be on the wrong side of.

Ron changed the subject. "Ready to jog again?"

"I can't keep up," Dennie smiled and sighed.

"Just slow down a little. With me near, you shall run and not be weary. You shall walk and not faint," Ron quoted from the Word of Wisdom section in the Doctrine and Covenants.

"Promise?" Dennie laughed. Ron Babcock was crazy. But as they began jogging, she followed his advice. She slowed down and struggled to breathe more evenly. Ron put his arm around her waist and ran with her. It made a huge difference. She could run more easily now. The rain was like a curtain parting for them with each step.

"Speaking of the children of Israel," Ron said, breathing easily. "You sounded great singing that song about Moses."

"Thanks," Dennie managed between huffs.

"I thought it was neat that it was dedicated to Thes and all."

"What?" Dennie's legs stiffened. She stopped running and pain lanced through her abdomen.

Ron moved his hand off Dennie's back. "You must not have heard because you were late. Your uncle said that although the song was about Moses, Thes had inspired it. Thes was a hero too. Thes gave his life to the Lord by dying in an effort to save Ty. Moses gave his life to the Lord by saving the children of Israel. Brother Taylor dedicated the song to Thes."

Another pain gripped Dennie. She hunched over.

"Are you all right?" She felt Ron's hand on her back once more.

"Just a cramp," Dennie lied. "Keep running. I'm going in."

Ron awkwardly loped away. Dennie shivered violently and forced herself to jog back towards the school. If she kept moving the cramp might go away. Soaking and shaking, she dragged herself into the locker room. She dropped onto a bench and put her head between her legs. The pain in her stomach lessened, but the cold penetrated every part of her. Then, she looked up. Through a high window, she noticed a hole in the clouds where the sun's rays slanted towards the earth.

CHAPTER 3

Raindrops Shattering on Stone

Two policemen woke us by prodding blunt sticks into our sides. Clumsy and dumb from sleep, we stumbled into the bed of a truck. I held Lautaro's hand and wet my filthy clothes. They dumped us at a jail where homeless children from the barrio were sheltered and fed during winter months.

I don't remember much of the jail. Someone with large hands washed me and pulled a sack-like dress over my head. I slept on a floor crowded with girls while my brother scrambled among the boys. I clung to him at mealtimes. Once he squatted and cupped a cricket in his palm. The insect beat against his hand, struggling for freedom. Lautaro asked me to pull out a strand of my hair. He wanted to tie it around the cricket's neck so he could keep it for a pet—like a dog on a leash. I told him "no." I didn't like people pulling out my hair! He scowled at me, his bushy eyebrows forming a dark V. Ignoring my request, he pulled out a long strand of my hair. He tied it around the cricket. When the cricket died, Lautaro wept.

One day, a Sister from the convent came. The nun's eyes latched onto me. She called to the mustached jail-man and announced that she would take me. I screamed for Lautaro. The man explained that he was my brother. The sister insisted he bring the boy to me to say good-bye.

But Lautaro would not say good-bye. He bit the woman's outstretched hand. He grabbed my shoulders and threw me into a corner of the room. With his arms outstretched like a tiny crucifix, he braced himself in front of me. He kicked and clawed anyone who came near. "He is well named," the jail-man said. "He has a lion's heart like the legendary Lautaro." Years later I found out that the legendary Lautaro was a young Mapuchi Indian who died fighting to liberate his people. But that day I only hoped that the jail-man's strange words would change the nun's mind. They didn't.

I remember how Lautaro scratched and bit the jail-man. The big man pinned Lautaro to the rough wall. I thought of the cricket. The man didn't want to hurt my brother, but he wouldn't let him free. I remember my shrieks and the acid sting of my tears as the Sister of Charity carried me away.

I slept on a cot in a small, stonewalled room near the convent's kitchen. I remember the smell of corn and fish, nights passing and raindrops shattering on stone. The nuns didn't slap me or yell at me. Instead they petted me and brought me sweets. Still, I wanted my brother. "Eat, child," they begged. "Speak to us, little Mina." I would not.

"Aim, I'm nervous!" Dennie moaned as she took the keys out of the ignition. Both girls descended from the Fletcher's Chevrolet Tahoe into the parking lot of the local fast-food restaurant, Farmer Owen's Beef Burgers. Aimy was dressed smartly in a short tan skirt and waist-length jacket.

"Come on, they'll hire us both!" Aimy squeezed Dennie's hand. "It'll be fun. We can help each other out. Cover for each other."

It was Tuesday afternoon. The sun shone illusively in the faded winter sky, while the wind bit through Dennie's sweater. Dennie thought about the reasons why she had decided to get a job. She didn't *need* the income like Aimy. Her parents gave her an ample allowance. They had always told her that grades were the priority, that school *was* her work. Years ago, they had set up a trust fund for her college education. But still, she had come. She had come because she hoped that working would empty her mind of everything except the immediate moment, that she would forget herself and feel a part of the world again. But as she and Aimy walked towards the door, Dennie felt these hopes might be illusions.

"What's bugging you? Are you really that nervous?" Aimy asked.

"Even if I get the job, my legs are too fat to wear those overall shorts they have for uniforms!" Dennie commented, feeling mildly surprised at the distance between her words and her thoughts.

"Nay, woman, you have small ankles and great calves," Aimy insisted.

"And cow thighs."

Aimy laughed. "Not true."

Dennie bit her lower lip. Aimy squared her shoulders. Aimy's eyes were bright points of determined blue, and the sharp angles of her jaw were firmly set. She flung the door open and Dennie followed her in.

The girls found Owen Hatcher, the owner, inspecting a bulletin board with a heading that read *Farmhands*. Pictures of the employees grinned benignly beneath the letters. They only recognized one, Sean Garrett. He was a guy in the ward who had recently returned from a mission. The bulletin board told them that he was now assistant manager. Owen turned when the girls approached.

"Welcome, welcome!" he grinned enthusiastically, displaying crooked, discolored teeth. Aimy grabbed Dennie's application form and stepped confidently forward. She handed over both sets of paperwork. As Owen surveyed the girls, his wire-rimmed glasses clouded with steam. His overalls hung limp and were splattered with grease. Dennie looked down for a moment. She focused on Owen's bulging feet stuffed into leather sandals. His thick white legs were covered with black fuzz. Thank heavens his socks covered his hairy toes.

"Sit down, sit down. I'll go over these in the office and be with you ladies in a nanosecond."

"We know Sean Garrett," Aimy interrupted, pointing to the picture. "He's great."

"That he is!" Owen smiled toothily at them. Then, he shuffled away.

Aimy swept over to a booth near the cattle mural. The bench seats, covered in red-and-white-checked plastic, squeaked as she sat down. Aimy pulled Dennie down beside her. "I hope we get this job!" Aimy exclaimed.

"I loved this place when I was little," Dennie said uncertainly, as she eyed the smiling cows painted on the opposite wall.

"Vision, Density! Someday Beef Burgers could be a worldwide chain! Just think, we could be transferred anywhere on the planet! We could end up making pig-tail curly fries in Tahiti!"

Dennie smiled thinly. A female employee with an overall strap drooping over one shoulder wiped up a nearby table. "Just what I've always wanted to be," Dennie remarked, "a farmhand wiping up Beef Burgers and melted Creamy Milkshakes."

"Shut up, Density!" Aimy suddenly hissed. "Don't blow it! Here comes Owen!"

"Ladies," Owen rubbed his hands together as he approached the girls. "I gave Sean a call. He had only good things to say. I'm impressed with you both. We're a big family here and I need girls like you! Start training on Thursday afternoon!"

"Perfect!" Aimy said. Dennie nodded and smiled.

"Now that you are farmhands," Owen added, "your first assignment is to get yourselves some overalls and shave those legs!" Owen wheezed with laughter.

On the way home, Dennie referred to Owen's comment, "Aim, don't you think that's sexual harassment?"

"Density, have you no sense of humor?" Aimy asked. She wheezed like Owen.

Dennie chuckled as she maneuvered the Tahoe around a bend in the road. She thought about how she was a good driver, smooth and consistent. Uncle Blake called her Queen of the Road.

"Den, what are you doing tonight?" Aimy asked.

"Blake and Karin are coming over for dinner. Want to come?" Dennie turned on the car's blinker and expertly pulled off Grantlin Boulevard into their neighborhood.

"No thanks. Brak is picking me up. He invited me to get something to eat," Aimy's calculated answer was smooth and nonchalant. Dennie jerked the car up into her driveway.

"Aim, don't get back together with him!"

"This is nothing. His parents are out of town and my mom is working late. He wanted company. He's changed, Dennie."

"I don't believe that."

"Dennie, you have a great family and a warm supper waiting for you. I don't have that. With Thes gone, you and Brak are about the only people who really care about me. I don't have backups; I can't afford to lose the people who care about me."

"Thes cared about you, but Brak doesn't. He only cares about himself." Dennie looked down at her hands.

"Thes is gone! He's not coming back!" Aimy burst out.

Dennie gripped the steering wheel so hard that her knuckles turned sharp and white. Moments passed. When Aimy spoke her voice was miserable, as if she were trying with her bare hands to dig a tunnel through Dennie's wall of angry silence. "I miss him too, Density. I miss him so much. I dream about him all the time. But it's my life!"

Time passed as Dennie blinked her eyes fiercely. She would not cry. It wouldn't help. Finally, she forced herself to relax one fist, then the other. She let go of the steering wheel. Her knuckles regained their smooth olive texture and color. "You're right," Dennie whispered. "My brother is gone. Nobody can change that."

The girls watched as Brak's dark-green '68 Mustang turned onto the street and stopped in front of Aimy's house. Brak glanced at Aimy's front door, honked the horn and drummed his long fingers against the black steering wheel.

"You better go," Dennie said. "The man's not known for his patience."

"He doesn't know we're here. He thinks I'm inside my house. It won't kill him to wait a minute," Aimy remarked. Aimy reached into the backseat to retrieve her backpack. Then she gave Dennie a hug. "I love ya, Density," she said.

"Me too, you," Dennie hugged her back.

When Aimy opened the car door, Brak turned his head and gazed at the Fletcher's blue Tahoe. Aimy jumped out of the car and ran toward him. Brak rolled his window down. "Hey, Fletcher!" Brak lifted up a hand in greeting to Dennie as Aimy climbed into his car.

Dennie remained silent. She had heard Brak Meyers yell those words before. *Hey, Fletcher!* He had once yelled at Thes. *Hey, Fletcher, stay away from Aimy or I'll kill you!*

"Honey, hi!" Meryl Fletcher met her daughter at the door with a warm embrace. But Dennie's body was stiff within the hug. Meryl stepped back a bit, and Dennie noticed that her mother covered her disappointment with a smile. It didn't used to be that way. There was a time when Dennie fit in her mother's arms. The house smelled of pot roast and mashed potatoes. "How'd the interview go?" Meryl Fletcher asked.

"I'm officially part of the work force," Dennie answered with as much enthusiasm as a limp carrot.

"That's my farmhand!" Rick Fletcher strode into the room. He hugged Dennie possessively.

"Dennie!" Karin Parker's voice rang from the kitchen. "I remember my first job! It was so fun!"

"Congratulations, Darling." Meryl Fletcher touched Dennie's hand for an instant before returning to the kitchen. *Mama, I feel so far away*, Dennie's thoughts cried. *I want to feel close to you again.*

Chris, Karin's seven-year-old son, bounded into the room, his blond hair catching the light as he hurtled over furniture and wrapped his arms around Dennie's waist, knocking her over with his back-wrenching-knock-the-wind-out crunch. Blake and Karin followed in his wake, their goal to undo whatever Chris had just done. In Dennie's case it nearly meant CPR.

"Christopher, settle down!" Karin exclaimed. "Dennie are you OK?" Dennie stood up, gasping. She nodded. After Dennie caught her breath, Karin explained. "He's Mowgli from Jungle Book. That was a python hug. He's excited for you, Den."

Blake picked Chris up, tossed him over his head and onto his back. "Me Tarzan. You Mowgli. Dennie home. Us eat."

Dennie followed her family into the dining room. The table was set with the lace tablecloth, the pale-green china with the tiny roses, and the salmon-colored linen napkins. "Why all the fuss?" Dennie asked as they sat down together. "This is just a stupid minimum-wage job."

Mom smiled gently. "We wanted to celebrate if you got the job and console you if you didn't. Besides, Karin and Blake did most of the cooking."

"It was our pleasure!" Karin beamed. Her bright hair hung soft and loose around her face.

"Let's kneel for family prayer," Dad invited. Dennie thought of how Thes had hated having family prayer right before meals. He had hated the waiting, the cold food. Whenever it had been Thes's turn, he had said the shortest prayers in the universe much to their father's chagrin. *Bless the food. Bless our family. In the name of Jesus Christ. Amen.*

Dennie knelt down and leaned with folded arms into the seat of the cherry-wood chair. She cradled her head feeling the rough nap of her sweater's sleeve against her cheek. Her father prayed, thanking the Lord for their blessings, for the food, for family and friends, for Blake, Karin and Chris, for their thoughtfulness and skill in preparing the meal. He thanked the Lord for Dennie and for her new job. He asked that she would enjoy it and be an example of good to others. Then he asked for comfort for the family as they missed Thes so much. His voice broke. He asked that they would find peace in knowing that Thes died trying to save a friend. He asked for joy to return to their home. He closed the prayer in the name of Jesus Christ.

After he finished, the family stood up and took their seats. Dennie watched her mother reach over and squeeze her father's hand. It was as if the gesture said, we will be OK, we will survive this, our lives will continue. Dennie sucked in a trembling breath much as a baby does in the silent instant before it screams. But Dennie couldn't scream. She was caught in the moment before the scream.

Only her silent thoughts screamed to her parents. Mama, Daddy, Thes didn't die trying to save a friend. He died because he was drunk. I knew about the cans of beer. I saw them in the car. I didn't tell you. I didn't stop him. Your son stumbled drunkenly out onto the rocks when the tide was high. Can't you see the wave rising like a mountain? Thes didn't hunker down and stand his ground. He just watched the wave rise and let the ocean swallow him. Brak told Aimy. I don't know how he found out. But I saw the beer. I knew Thes drank. If I had told you, you would have stopped him. If I had told you, he would still be alive. But now Ty has lied, and you've found meaning in Thes's death. You're pushing your heads up out of the water, above the grief. If I told you the truth, what would happen? Would sorrow swallow you like the wave swallowed Thes? Would you hate me as much as I hate Ty?

"Dennie, are you all right?" Her mother's voice pierced Dennie's thoughts like a needle puncturing a balloon.

"Sure," Dennie said.

"Have some mashed potatoes," her father handed them to her. As the dinner progressed, Dennie saw the people she loved smiling at her, reaching out to her with words, looks, and gestures. They wanted her to respond, to need them, to be with them, to grieve less, to drink out of the cup of life fully once more. Dennie knew this and so she filled her plate with roast, potatoes, gravy, and peas. She thanked Karin for making double-fudge chocolate brownies, her favorite dessert. But to Dennie, their acts of kindness felt like raindrops shattering on stone.

CHAPTER 4

White Moonlight

*One day the priest came to see me. As he spoke, he blinked his watery
eyes that looked as if they had been washed shiny by a thousand tears. The
next morning the sisters dressed me in pink and pinned a bow in my hair.
They told me that the priest had decided that I would not stay. I would go
on an airplane to the United States.*

*A man in a suit waited in a car. The silvery rain patted on the
umbrella held by the Nun. I cringed into her skirts until I realized that
the strange, clean child in the backseat had Lautaro's smile. I raced into
the car. It was my brother! He wore new clothes and shiny black shoes. I
touched his shoes. I touched his face—so clean and smelling of soap. He
laughed and tugged at my bow. I slapped his fingers. He grabbed my
hand and held it tightly. "I didn't forget you, Mina," he said. "Every day,
I told the jail-man to bring you back."*

*The man driving the car took us to the airport. Inside the terminal,
he bought us candy bars in bright metallic wrappers. I bit into mine. The
outside was chocolate, the inside so sweet and soft. We sat down to wait.
The man said he was our tio, our Uncle Blake. I thought Lautaro would
laugh at his joke. Anyone could tell he was not our uncle with his skin
pale as a scar, his thin stringy hair the color of brown rice, and his eyes as
blue as a flower.*

*He explained that once he lived in Chile as a Mormon missionary.
The jail-man was his friend. Tio Blake had come back to Chile to find a
child for his sister and her husband to adopt. But he found Lautaro and
Mina, two children instead of one! Tio Blake said that God, Our Father
in Heaven, made this possible. His sister and her husband wanted us
both! We would live in the United States. They would be our parents. He*

would take us on an airplane to meet them. Did we understand? I copied Lautaro's nod.

We finished the candy and licked our fingers. He handed us a picture. "Your mama and papa," he said. The woman in the picture had pants that went down to her knees; her pink legs looked too skinny to hold her up. Her wheat-colored hair was chopped short. Her teeth were large and white like a rabbit's. The man's arm stretched around her shoulders. His hair and eyes were the color of honey. He wore glasses. His nose was large and his teeth were straight and small. Lautaro smiled at the couple in the picture, then asked Tio Blake for more candy please.

The airplane reminded me of the candy bar, wrapped in bright metal with surprises inside: soft seats, dove-white pillows, sweet-smelling blankets. I hid my face in Lautaro's shoulder as the metal ship pointed its body into the dark clouds. Lautaro laughed as we broke into the blue, above the dark-laced clouds, safe now from the wind and rain. He shrugged me away and put his arms out like wings and made bird and airplane sounds. He had finally won the race! He was faster than the sky!

I began crying. Tio Blake put his big hand on my knee and said, "Mina, don't be frightened. I'm here to take care of you. I'm your friend." When I stopped crying I asked Uncle Blake if the Father in Heaven might change his mind. Couldn't this airplane fly me to heaven and my dead mama instead of to strangers in the United States? Tio Blake shook his head. "No, Mina, I'm sorry." He patted my knee and smiled at me, but I saw tears balancing in his flower-blue eyes.

I'll have a Bacon Beef Burger, one Creamy Chocolate Milkshake, and a large order of Pig-tail Fries."

___ "Will that be all?"

"No. There's one more thing. When do you get off work?" Dennie ignored Ty Edwards's question as he tried to make eye contact with her. She stared at the cash register and punched in his order.

"Five fifty-seven please," she said barely looking at him.

"You get off at five fifty-seven?"

"No. Five dollars and fifty-seven cents. Is this order to go?"

"I'm eating here." Ty handed the money to Dennie. His fingers were large and square like the rest of him. Any stranger would have thought that Dennie, with her long French braid and striking black eyes, had never seen Ty before. She was so quick and indifferent as she tapped the price out on the cash register, taking his bill and giving him change without so much as a finger brushing his hand. She must be in love with someone else, they would have thought, for it didn't take a genius or sage to notice the frustration in the boy's voice or the look of angry longing in his eyes as he spoke to the girl.

"Why won't you talk to me?" Ty grabbed Dennie's wrist as she handed him his order.

"I'm at work. I have a customer waiting," Dennie's eyes momentarily met his.

"I can wait here until you're off. I'll give you a ride home. I need to explain some things."

"Aimy's giving me a ride home. I've got to go." Dennie pulled her wrist away and moved back to her station. She smiled at the next person in line, but there wasn't a hint of sparkle in her black eyes.

During Dennie's break, she watched Aimy wipe up the tables. Her friend charmed the customers, her slim legs flashing with energy as she worked. They had only been working two weeks and Owen had already given Aimy a raise. She was his prodigy, the farmhand of his dreams. But Dennie knew that Aimy's energy and flair were surface. Inside, Aimy's thoughts ticked like seconds slipping from a clock. Each ten minutes of her shift broke down into a dollar, a dollar towards a bill, a dollar towards a new dress, a dollar towards a loaf of bread, each dollar chipping off a bit of the load piled on her slim shoulders.

At eight-thirty that night, after they left work, Aimy asked Dennie if she wanted to drop by the youth dance. "Sure," Dennie responded.

"Ronny-boy will be there," Aimy mentioned. "He might ask one of us out. During seminary, whenever I look at him, he's already looking at us."

"You sure?" Dennie asked.

"Sure, I'm sure," Aimy mimicked. "Then, when he notices me noticing that he's staring our way, his ears turn all red." Aimy laughed as she hit the brakes. The car shuddered to a halt just before the stop sign. She gunned it when it was her turn to go. Dennie thought about how Aimy drove—skidding stops, screeching starts.

But although Aimy seemed like an aggressive driver, she was inconsistent. She was afraid to turn left into traffic. She would swing the car into a neighborhood, and race around a block, just to avoid turning left.

"Ronny-boy is lucky," Aimy went on. "He has such a perfect family. Last Sunday I had an interview with his dad. Bishop Babcock asked me why I haven't been coming to Mutual lately. I told him I have too much homework and I'm working and stuff. Then he promised to postpone the biology test until Friday if I promised to take Tuesday off and go to Mutual. I told him I'd think about it. Then, on Monday, Mr. Babcock—you know, the bishop who morphs into a biology teacher, announced to the class that the test would be Friday instead of Wednesday. He winked at me like we had this huge secret. It was so funny. Bishop Babcock is the nicest dork, just like Ronny-boy. I think we should skip the dance and TP their house. Do you want to?"

"Sure," Dennie shrugged.

"Sure. Sure. Sure. Density, you have quite the extensive vocabulary tonight. Let's stop by Ed's Grocery for the toilet paper. Do you have a couple of bucks?"

"Sure," Dennie said purposely. Aimy laughed and shook her head.

"Hopeless! Hopeless!" Aimy turned at the light, then flew down the alley in order to avoid turning left onto Grantlin Boulevard.

Ten minutes later the car was loaded with toilet paper and they were on their way to the Babcocks in East Grantlin. While Aimy drove, Dennie thought about how she and Aimy had never before toilet papered without Thes. For years, they called themselves the TPT, the toilet-papering-trio. They used to strike once a month, on Friday evenings, while the Fletcher parents were at the temple. Dennie had always volunteered to be the lookout. She liked being close enough to feel the excitement, but not close enough to get in trouble, to risk getting caught. That had left Aimy and Thes with the dirty work, only they called it their art work, their masterpieces. Dennie could still picture the way they threw the rolls of toilet paper over and around the trees and bushes, the streamers flying like ribbons in the wind, Aimy's hair white in the moonlight and Thes's black. In the silent pantomime, their hands had waved, clapped, communicated, as their feet ran and skipped. Sometimes, it had seemed almost like they were dancing, almost like they were in love.

Dennie remembered the last time they had gone together, the fall night when the moon had been full and low. Their escapade had been interrupted. Unknown to the trio, Brak Meyers had parked down the street and had watched his girlfriend and Thes Fletcher TP the coach's house. Aimy had slipped and fallen on the damp grass. Thes had raced to her, sliding down beside her. When Aimy had attempted to scramble to her feet, Thes had pulled her back down and had wrapped toilet paper around her. They had struggled on the ground, laughing voicelessly, trying to wrap each other in toilet paper that was so white it nearly glowed. Alone in the driver's seat of the Tahoe, Dennie had been the first to see Brak's car drive toward Aimy and Thes. She had screamed and honked as the Mustang leapt over the curb onto the coach's lawn. Thes had jumped to his feet and pushed Aimy away from the oncoming headlights. It had stopped just a few inches from him. With fists clenched and dripping with shreds of toilet paper, Thes had blinked while drenched in the brightness of the car's lights. Brak had rolled down the window and yelled, "Hey, Fletcher, stay away from Aimy or I'll kill you! Fletcher, I'll be watching you!"

Then Brak had peeled away, leaving the coach's lawn scarred and Aimy weeping. "He didn't mean it, Thessie," Aimy had cried. "He could never kill anything. He just gets mad sometimes."

Later that night, as Dennie had driven them home, Thes had asked through clenched teeth, "Why don't you break up with him?"

"Thessie, I can't. He loves me." Aimy's voice had been small and vulnerable, a shadow of its vibrant self.

"Density, wake up! We're here. And we're in luck. The house is dark." Aimy's sharp whisper brought Dennie back into the moment. Aimy stopped the car in front of the Babcocks's home.

"Density, you can't be lookout tonight. You have to help me with the toilet paper." Aimy reached into the backseat and grabbed a roll.

"Aim, maybe we should park down the street so we can run for it if someone shows up."

"No one's home. Let's just hurry and do it, then we can go to the dance and play innocent."

Dennie started to open the car door, then hesitated. "Aimy, maybe we shouldn't. Do you think the Babcocks would mind?"

"Density, don't be Chicken Little." Aimy opened the door soundlessly, habitually pushed the lock button, and silently closed it. Dennie thought of the countless times, when they were small, that Thes had called her Chicken Little. She was sick of being afraid, sick of how much Thes had hurt her by dying.

In defiance, Dennie grabbed a roll of toilet paper and jumped out of the car, shutting the door as she flung the roll toward the nearest evergreen, a young cone-shaped redwood. Instead of unraveling, it hit the Redwood like a baseball and lodged in a joint of trunk and branch. Aimy cracked up, "Density, I need to give you lessons on the art of toilet paper throwing!"

Suddenly, a dog's angry barks split the night. "Shh! We're making too much noise!" Dennie giggled.

"If you weren't such a klutz," Aimy whispered. Then, the dog threw itself against the gate leading into the Babcocks's backyard. The force of the animal's body pushed the gate open.

"Time to get in the car," Dennie said as a Doberman emerged, barking furiously. Dennie took hold of the door handle, but it was locked.

"I can't find the keys!" Aimy's voice sounded high and frightened as her hands bobbed in and out of her pockets, searching. Aimy had always been terrified of dogs.

The dog growled as it approached. Aimy vaulted onto the hood and scrambled to the roof of the car.

Dennie didn't move, but it wasn't because she felt frozen in fear. Dennie had always loved animals. She felt drawn to them. She knew the dog might bite her, but it would be due to instinct, not evil.

"Dennie, please! Climb up here!" Aimy cried from on top of the car. The fear in her friend's voice reached Dennie through the darkness of the night and the barking of the dog.

"Aim, it's OK. I met this dog at a fireside once. I don't think it will hurt us." Dennie squatted down and cupped both hands, one close to her body and the other reaching towards the animal, beckoning the dog to her. "Come here, sweetheart, come here. I won't hurt you." Dennie's voice was low and kind, addressing the dog as if it could understand every word. "I know this is your house. I won't hurt anything. I promise. Come sit by me." She whistled softly.

The dog stopped barking and studied Dennie tensely. Then, as Dennie continued talking to the dog, the lines of the animal's body slowly softened and its stub-like tail began moving back and forth in a hesitant wag. Dennie called the dog once more. It trotted to her, lowering its head subserviently. Dennie reached up and tenderly stroked its ears. She touched the dog's face gently, enjoying its sleek, black softness.

"I hate to interrupt this Kodak moment, but I see the keys on the pavement next to the door," Aimy called from the roof.

"Come on down," Dennie suggested as she stroked the dog.

"Why don't you take the nice doggie into the backyard first?" Aimy suggested.

"Chicken Little." Dennie grinned, rubbing it in. Aimy was about to respond when the headlights of an approaching car interrupted her. Dennie stiffened, remembering once more the night when Brak's car roared toward Aimy and Thes. The Doberman next to Dennie wiggled in excitement as the Honda stopped behind Aimy's car.

The headlights flicked off. Bishop and Ron Babcock hurtled out. "Girls, are you all right?" the Bishop asked anxiously. About as inconspicuously as an earthquake, Aimy slid down from the roof of the car. She dusted off her pants. "We're fine," she said with a charming smile. "We just stopped by to see if Ron wanted to go to the dance with us. Your dog sort of scared us."

Ron raised his eyebrows. "This is a pleasant surprise, but Dennie doesn't look too scared."

"She's one of those canine people," Aimy explained.

The bishop peered at the girls through his glasses. "I'm relieved. We were at the dance when a neighbor called the church. She said the dog was loose and that a couple of teenagers were making a ruckus outside the house."

"Well, it was just us. Sorry. We better get going or we'll miss the rest of the dance," Aimy chirped spryly.

"Hang on a minute, girls, I have something in the house for you." Bishop Babcock lumbered towards the front door. As he unlocked the door, his image looked like a dark, tall shadow, with a kindly softness and slightly stooping shoulders.

"So you two came to pick me up for the dance." Ron's voice swaggered a bit as he spoke to the girls.

"Yea, Ronny-boy, we were in need of entertainment," Aimy made eye contact.

"I can supply that. Let me take care of Gretchen first."

"Gretchen?" Dennie questioned.

Ron smiled at her. "My dog."

Dennie scratched the Doberman's ears. "See ya later, Gretchen."

Ron whistled for the dog while striding toward the gate. As Gretchen ran to him, she brushed against the lower branches of the redwood tree where the toilet paper was lodged. Aimy and Dennie looked at each other, suppressing giggles, wondering if the toilet paper would fall. It held.

Ron came back into the front yard as Bishop Babcock emerged on the front steps. The Bishop carried a brown paper grocery bag with the top folded down. He handed the bag to Dennie. "Open it later, girls," he smiled as he winked at both of them. "Consider it an exchange." Then he walked to his Honda. He turned and waved before getting in. "See you kids at the dance." Bishop Babcock bumped his head as he lowered himself into the car.

"What'd my dad give you?" Ron asked as he playfully grabbed the bag and opened it. "Hey, there's a plate of cookies in here and a roll of toilet paper. Why on earth would my dad give you a roll of toilet paper?"

"Because he's the nicest dork," Aimy said.

"I don't get it. Did you Fletchers borrow toilet paper from us or something?" Ron shook his head. Dennie heard Gretchen bark in the backyard. She realized that the dog's coat was shiny black, much like Thes's hair. In her mind, she pictured Aimy and Thes throwing toilet paper through moonlight. She remembered two different sets of headlights. She saw her roll lodged in the tree. She looked down at the roll in her bag. Gretchen barked again like she wanted to come out and play.

Then, for some unknown reason, Dennie began laughing. She doubled over in the moonlight, her laughter uncontrolled, rushing out of her like water bursting from a dam. Aimy giggled, but Dennie's outburst haunted her, for it was so unlike Dennie to laugh like that and so much like Thes. But, if Thes had been there, he would have known that his sister's strange laughter was only a shade away from relentless weeping. While, to Ron Babcock, it was the most wonderful sound in the world.

CHAPTER 5

Dance with Me Forever

I awakened as the airplane landed. I rubbed my eyes. We stepped through the door into a long tunnel. The mother and father in the photo waited at the end of the tunnel. They looked like a picture standing there, cut out from a magazine and pasted in the gray airport. As we drew nearer I noticed that the woman had the same flower-blue eyes as Tio Blake. She broke loose from the picture. She ran to us. She cried as she gathered Lautaro and me to her. She told us her name was Meryl Fletcher. She was our new mommy. She took our hands and led us to Rick Fletcher, our father. He reached out to us like he wanted to hug us, but instead he touched my cheek and patted Lautaro's shoulder. On the way home, the woman sat in the back seat with Lautaro and me. She held my hand.

Our new house had so much food! It smelled clean like soap. There were soft carpets, smooth floors, and the telephone was hooked up to a machine that talked. There was a swing set in the backyard. In my room the furniture was white like heaven. On my bed there was a thick quilt with the image of a fluffy white kitten framed in the center by small even stitches. A doll sat on my dresser. She had dark eyes and olive skin like mine.

I liked our new home. My mother hugged me when I cried, and made French toast in the mornings. Her pink freckled nose, toothy smile, and kind blue eyes became so familiar to me. Soon, they seemed to be the eyes of the only mother I'd ever known.

In the center of the downstairs was a special room, called a den. It looked as if the walls were made of books. A computer and a printer rose from a smooth desk that was crowded with papers. Every morning after breakfast Mommy led us to the den and we sat on a velvet sofa the color of chocolate. She read to us from books with striking bright drawings and words we couldn't understand. First she would point to the pictures and tell us the names of things. Then, she would read the stories. As she continued, we came to understand the words and the patterns. After a time, the English language filled our minds and joined our dreams.

But Lautaro warned me to never go in the den at night. He told me that the dead people who wrote the books walked in the den at night. "This house has too many rooms," Lautaro said. "Too many places for ghosts." But although I was afraid of many things, I wasn't afraid of ghosts like Lautaro. Ghosts were made of air. They couldn't hurt you like people who were alive.

One night I couldn't sleep. The moon was a wedge of light and the summer breeze made the blinds shiver. Earlier that day my brother had called me a baby. I would prove that I was braver than Lautaro. I would find a ghost. I silently slid from the bed. I stepped into the den as softly as a kitten. I sat on the dark sofa and waited.

A light flickered in the hallway. "Mina?" I heard Mommy's whisper as she came down the hall with a flashlight. "What are you doing?"

"Waiting. The ghosts of the dead people who wrote these books come here at night. If I see them, Lautaro will know I am not a baby."

"But I am the only writer who comes here at nights," Mommy explained as she turned on the lamp. "And I am still alive. Mina, did you know that I wrote a poem in one of these books?"

She took a book from the shelf. It was called "Bright Days—A Collection of Poems for the Very Young." Mommy opened to a page and smiled. "My only published poem," she said.

The picture on the page was of a little girl with yellow hair sitting under a tree with orange leaves. "Sitting under the Liquidambar tree," Mommy read, "bright sea star leaves smile down on me. Together they whisper, 'Let's play with the wind.' I grin and grin and grin and grin. By Meryl Fletcher." Mommy pointed to her name on the page.

I spelled 'Meryl' aloud, remembering the names of all the letters. "You little genius!" Mommy exclaimed as she hugged me. "Now come upstairs." That night I slept in my parents' bed with them. My head fit perfectly within the crook of my mother's arm.

But for Lautaro it was different. There were not only too many rooms in the house, but too many rules as well. Regardless of how hard he tried, more rules were thrown at him, like small irritating pebbles hitting him over and over again: Eat at the table! Take your shoes off before walking on the carpet! Leave the landscaping rocks where they are! Don't go farther than the court! Don't paint your face with mud! Never climb the fence into the neighbor's yard! Stay out of the garbage can, and never, ever, play with the kitchen knives!

Also, Lautaro couldn't stop stealing food. He'd hide it under his pillow, in the wastebasket, beneath his bed, inside the clothes in his drawers. Sometimes, he would forget about the food and his room would stink.

One day, the rotten food under a pile of clothes stained the carpet green. Lautaro was with me in my room when Daddy discovered it. After trying unsuccessfully to scrub it out, Daddy called to Mom. "Meryl!" He shouted down the stairs. We heard Mom hurry up the stairs to see what was wrong.

"Look at this! I can't get the stain out! The carpet's ruined!" Daddy's voice was angry. "Why can't he stop! We give him all he wants to eat! He needs to know that we won't put up with this. Where is he?"

"Don't talk to him until you cool down!" Mommy's voice was stern. "We've never been hungry. We don't know what it does to kids."

"Mina was hungry too! She never sneaks or lies. I don't understand why he won't stop!"

"Rick, be patient!" Mommy shouted back.

"Meryl, you're always making excuses for his actions. He needs to understand consequences, to learn to be responsible."

I looked at Lautaro. He stared at the floor. Then he looked up at me and his eyes told me of his hurt. I hugged my dark-eyed doll. I felt afraid. Didn't they understand that I never had to sneak or lie? Whenever I was hungry I knew it would end. I knew it would end because I had a brother. I had a brother who would bring me food. I had a brother who raced the sky.

But no matter what Lautaro did, Mommy was patient. During the evenings when Daddy worked late, she would turn on the stereo and encourage us to dance. I wasn't quick on my feet like Lautaro. How he loved to dance with her! They would dance to Garth Brooks, Elton John, and The Beach Boys. Lautaro would shake when they did the macarena and listen carefully to Mommy's instructions when she led him in a waltz.

Mommy would laugh and say, "After Daddy and I were married, your father quit dancing with me. Now I have someone to dance with me forever!"

On the way to the dance, Dennie twisted around in the front seat to look at Ron. "Tell me about Gretchen," she said.

"My sister, Elise, found her abandoned when she was a puppy. What else do you want to know?"

Aimy interrupted. "I want to know why anyone would name a man-eating Doberman *Gretchen*? You should have named her *Killer* or something."

"Elise named her. Why are you prejudiced against Dobermans, Aimy? She's a great dog." Ron commented. Aimy shrugged.

"How long have you had her?" Dennie asked.

"Two years. Mike Carlo, Sister Allen's son, helped Elise train her."

"Are Mike and your sister still together?" Aimy asked.

Ron shrugged. "Sort of. But Elise's also writing a missionary she dated at BYU. Elise is flying home for Presidents' Day and Mike's going to be in Grantlin that weekend. I think she's coming home to see *him*, not us."

It was quiet in the car for a moment as Aimy waited at a stop sign for a chance to turn left onto Grantlin Boulevard. Aimy tapped the steering wheel with her fingernails. She blinked her eyes nervously.

"You can go now," Ron quipped.

"I know that," Aimy retorted as she peeled out.

At the dance, Ron hung around Aimy and Dennie. The three moved casually to the music as they talked.

"So, Ronny-boy, what's it like having a perfect Beaver Cleaver family?" Aimy asked during the final half-hour of the dance.

"We're not perfect," Ron said. "But, hey, I'm an uncle. Sarah's baby, Jolyn, turned one this week."

"I remember when Sarah used to baby-sit Thes and me," Dennie commented.

"So tell me one way that your family isn't perfect?" Aimy challenged.

"Last week my little sister, Tammy, tried to buy toys over the Internet with my parents' Visa number."

Aimy laughed. "Your little sister is so adorable. I would give anything to have a little sister to take care of and a big brother to look out for me."

Ron grinned. "Come on. It must be great being an only child. You always get the car. There aren't dirty towels all over the bathroom floor. Your mom never calls you the wrong name."

"Ronny-boy," Aimy said seriously, "sometimes there is nothing worse than being an only child."

A strangled sound escaped Dennie before she could stop it. She felt Ron and Aimy's eyes on her. Her face burned. Did they know what she was thinking—that the only thing worse than being an only child was having a brother, and then losing him? Her eyes stung with unshed tears and she was afraid that if she began crying, she would never stop.

"Come on, Dennie," Ron said. "This is the last song. Dance with me." He took her in his arms. As Dennie's cheek rested on Ron's shoulder, he wished the dance would last forever.

CHAPTER 6

Names

I used to think that names were just words representing people; and they simply filled a void, finding their meaning in the people they labeled. Not anymore. Now, I think that names change people. You hear your name over and over, the sound and tone of the syllables, the memory of its meaning. It's like ceaseless waves lapping the coastline, changing its shape forever.

About six months after we came to America, Daddy bought Lautaro and me new bikes. Lautaro's was shiny black, flecked with purple. It had deep rutted tires. Mine was pink with a horn that honked when I squeezed a rubber ball. I admired my bike from a distance like you admire a quarter sparkling in a fountain. But I was afraid to touch it or ride it. I knew I would fall. Daddy said he understood. He screwed on training wheels. Then, Mommy walked next to me as I slowly pedaled down the sidewalk.

With Lautaro it was different. His eyes shone like coals when he saw his new bike. Daddy showed him what to do and instantly Lautaro rode. It was as if he and the bike were one. He shot through the dusty field down the street. He laughed and shouted challenges to the clouds. He crouched down on his bike and swept through mud puddles. His leg muscles pumped with power and pride. He was the wind and the storm. He was king.

Then, his sandal strap caught in the spokes. I remember the thump of his helmet hitting the pavement. By the time we got to him he was sitting up. Blood spilled from his ankle. He shook his head in disbelief, but he didn't cry. Mommy swallowed, and Daddy carried him to the house. Lautaro looked back at me. "Mina, get my bike!" he screamed feverishly. I tried to stand it up and pull it, but it fell. I tried to drag it, but it was too heavy. While Mommy wiped the blood from my brother's leg and bound it with a towel, Daddy came back outside and helped me with the bike. Then, Mommy said that we needed to take Lautaro to the doctor's for stitches. Lautaro's eyes narrowed until both eyebrows formed a long bushy caterpillar. He refused to go anywhere without his bike. Reluctantly, Daddy loaded his bike into the back of the car.

I held Lautaro's hand while the doctor looked at his wound. I started to cry when I saw the needle they would use to sew his cut closed. "Don't cry, Mina," Lautaro grinned at me. "The sky doesn't think I can win. But now I have a bike."

Lautaro didn't cry when the nurse gave him a shot. He didn't whimper when the doctor stitched him up. But he squeezed my hand harder than usual, so hard that my palm bled a little where his fingernails had been.

On Monday night, a few weeks later, when we had all gathered in the den for family home evening, I noticed that the setting sun hung in the sky as red as Lautaro's blood. Mommy sat on the sofa with Lautaro and me. Daddy balanced on the two back legs of the desk chair.

"I have great news!" Daddy announced, "Your adoptions will be final in a few months. We need to talk about your names so I can finish up the paper work. Then we can go to the temple and be sealed together forever."

"Daddy and I are so happy!" Mommy said as she squeezed both of our shoulders.

Daddy's voice leapt to his question, "Do you want to keep the same first names, Mina and Lautaro, or do you want new American names? Your last name will be Fletcher, like ours."

"It's fine with us if you don't want to change your names. Or you can choose new names and keep Mina and Lautaro as middle names," Mommy commented almost shyly.

Lautaro and I were silent. It seemed so strange, this choosing of names. Aren't you just who you are?

"Some names mean things," Mommy said as she pulled a book of names off the shelf. She opened it. "See, here's my name, Meryl. It means 'bright sea.' And Daddy's name, Rick, means 'powerful ruler.'" Daddy flexed his muscles. Lautaro and I laughed.

Mommy began reading a list of names. When we didn't respond, she said, "Mina, you could be named after something, like 'summer' or 'autumn.'"

"I want to be named 'Den' after this room," I said.

Lautaro rolled his eyes and shook his head like I was hopeless.

Mom flipped through the book. "Let me see: Denise, Denizen. Denizen means at home in a new place." Mom spoke gently with a light in her eyes. She touched my hand. Her fingers were as soft as the petals of a flower. "That's perfect. Denizen. Denizen Mina Fletcher. Den or Dennie for short."

I grinned. Daddy picked me up and swung me around. "Denizen, my little Dennie," he sang. "The most beautiful girl in the world!" I laid my head on Daddy's shoulder. I felt the hardness of his muscles. There was a compactness about him, a sense of energy and exactness. Yet, as he sat me down, I knew there was a soft spot inside, for me.

I think Lautaro was jealous because he rushed to his feet. He grabbed his favorite book off the shelf. It was a picture book about the Greek hero, Theseus. In the book Theseus defeated the minotaur and found his way through the labyrinth. "Name me after him!" Lautaro grinned as he pointed to the picture of the muscle-bound Theseus. In the picture, the hero was wearing a toga and brandishing a sword. I giggled at the thought of Lautaro dressed like that.

Daddy shook his head. "I don't think so. When you start school, kids will laugh at you."

"Only this name." My brother shook his head back at Daddy who was eyeing Mommy like he needed help.

"Theseus Lautaro Fletcher," Mommy said questioningly to Daddy. "We could call him Thes for short."

Daddy looked at Mommy doubtfully. Then, Mommy did the strangest thing. She stood up and jumped up and down like a spastic cheerleader, her thin arms waving. "Thes, Thes, he's the best. He's much better than all the rest."

"My name! My name!" Lautaro roared, laughing. Daddy gave in. Thus, Thes and Dennie Fletcher were born.

"Let's stop by Beef Burgers," Aimy said as she pulled the car out of the church parking lot. "Owen wasn't finished making out paychecks when we left. They should be in our boxes now. It'll be closing time but Sean Garrett will still be there cleaning up and listening to COUNTRY FM 105. You know Sean, Ronny-boy? He got back from his mission to South Carolina in January. Now, he's a good old southern boy. He won't care if we make milkshakes. What will it be, Cowboy Ron, a Peanut Butter Crunch Creamy Milkshake or a Blue COW Glacial Freeze?"

"Well, shoot pie, Aimy. A boy like me just cain't make up his mind," Ron drawled.

Aimy laughed out loud. "Shucky darn, Ronny-boy, life's full of tough choices. Ain't it!"

Dennie smiled to herself. She liked the effect Ron had on Aimy, the way his wholesomeness seemed to soften her sarcasm. With Ron Babcock around it almost felt like everything would be normal again. Demons couldn't touch the wide, brightness of his smile. She took a deep breath and leaned back. Ron leaned forward in the back seat and put his hands around Dennie's head, massaging her forehead. Dennie sighed. She felt heavy-limbed and light-headed.

"I'm smoothing out the lumps in your brain," Ron said.

"Too bad you don't have more time," Aimy said as she swerved into the Beef Burger parking lot. "She's got lots of lumps."

A moment later, Sean opened the door with a smile that stretched the extent of his face. "Hey, it's the Teen Trio," he greeted them. "Aimy told me y'all might be back trying to get high on milkshakes." He snapped the dishtowel at Aimy.

Aimy grabbed a huge plastic ketchup bottle and attempted to squirt Sean in the stomach while dodging his towel snaps. "No one messes with the Teen Trio," she teased. Then, Sean grabbed Aimy's arm and stripped the ketchup bottle from her. "Death to the Teen Trio!" he yelled. Aimy backed away from him and ran towards Dennie and Ron. "Come on!" She grabbed their arms and pulled them through the side door. Sean squirted a stream of ketchup at them as they retreated into the parking lot.

An instant later, Sean came out waving a white dishtowel and calling for a truce. "Hey," he laughed. "Come back in! I'll make y'all milkshakes."

Aimy danced to Shania Twain and Faith Hill while she drank her milkshake. Sean joined in, dancing with the mop as he cleaned the floor. Dennie and Ron took their milkshakes into the dining area. They drank them in the dark under the smiling cows.

"Dennie," Ron asked. "Are you doing anything tomorrow night?"

"No. How come?"

"Dad, Tammy, and I are going to the Kings game and have an extra ticket. Want to come with us?"

Dennie was thoughtful for a moment. Thes had loved the Kings. Last year, when they were losing, he had been so frustrated. He'd screamed at them when they were on TV. *Stay in the paint! Don't gun it from outside! Quit throwing bricks!* This year the Kings had a shot at the playoffs. Thes would have been ecstatic.

"Well?" Ron asked.

"Sure," Dennie said softly. "It sounds fun."

Ron swallowed, "OK. We'll pick you up at 6:10."

"OK," Dennie nodded. Ron wondered if the sound of the wind outside was loud enough to cover the beating of his heart.

When Dennie arrived home, her mother was sitting in the living room. She looked up as Dennie walked into the room. Her fair complexion was splotchy and red. "Mom, are you OK?" Dennie asked.

"I didn't know where you were," Meryl Fletcher responded.

"Aimy and I went to the dance. Then, afterwards, we got shakes at Beef Burgers with Ron Babcock."

"Why didn't you call me and tell me where you were?" This wasn't like her mother: the battered tone of voice, the strange, almost accusing look in her eyes.

"Mom, I told you Aimy and I would call if we didn't go to the dance."

"But, Dennie, you weren't home by 11:15. The dance was over. I called the church and nobody answered. It's 12:15, Denizen. I didn't know where you were. Why didn't you call me?"

"Mom, I thought it was OK," Dennie explained. "My curfew is 12:00. I'm just a few minutes late. I didn't know you would be worried."

Her mother rubbed her face with her hands. Her mouth twisted uncontrollably as she spoke. "Dennie, try to understand. Just a little while before we got the call about Thes. Just a little while before, I thought about how much fun he must be having. I thought about what a beautiful day it was at the ocean. I thought about how bright the sea must have looked. But he was already gone. Tonight, I didn't know where you were. I didn't know what had happened to you. I didn't know if you were all right."

A sob rose from Meryl Fletcher. She covered her face with her hands and wept. Dennie stared at her. Where was her mother, that incredible woman who was clumsy and graceful at the same time, whose smile was as warm as the sun? Who was this woman, this sobbing mass of pain and anger? She needed a daughter, a daughter to hold her in her arms and weep with her. But Dennie could only stand there numbly, struggling to keep the weight of her guilt from knocking her down.

Her father came into the room. "Meryl," he said gently. "It's late. Dennie's home. She's fine. We all need to go to bed." He put his arm around his wife and led her out of the room.

Dennie turned around. The photo-poetry album about Thes lay open on the coffee table. Her mother must have been looking through it while she waited. Dennie looked at the picture of Thes taken at their first trip to the ocean. He was grinning crazily and holding a superman kite. The words of the poem next to the picture crowded in Dennie's mind, each word like a weight.

Oh! The trio
Kite, wind, and child!
What they can do!

Thes
Seven years old
Stern concentration
Bending
Lifting
Feeling the tug
Of String.
Directing, demanding
It soars

Heavenward.
On this sun-drenched seaside day
Together they defy—laugh at
Gravity.

Oh! The wonder of my son—
The physical prowess, the bright
Brilliance of muscle and brain.
How thankful I am for the aerodynamic divinity of
Kite construction.
And still I must give credit to
The wind.

When Rick Fletcher came back downstairs, his daughter was sitting stiffly on the sofa with the photo album lying on her lap like something dead. Her body looked so rigid that he didn't think it possible that she was sleeping; yet, her eyes were closed as if she had pulled the shades down over her soul. He stood next to her. "Dennie," he said, "your mother is tired tonight. She's overwrought. She overreacted. I'm sorry."

When she didn't respond, he found himself pleading. "Dennie, please talk to me. Thes is gone and now you're shutting us out. We need you."

"I'm sorry," she whispered. Then, she opened her eyes and the look of naked loneliness in them hit her father so hard that he had to place his hands upon her head to keep from reeling. And with his hands there he gave her a blessing, a blessing beseeching the powers of heaven to return light and laughter to his child. Then, he picked her up, cradling her in his arms. And as her father carried Dennie up the stairs to her room, she saw her black hair fall across his white T-shirt like a stain.

CHAPTER 7

Balance

In my dream my parents try to pull me out of dark water. I clutch their arms and shoulders but this makes us go deeper and deeper. We need to breathe. I know I must let go of them, even push them away so the water can buoy us up. But I can't! I can't stop pulling them down no matter how much I want to. Why am I in the black water? Did I fall? Then, I remember. I fell into the water while searching for Thes.

I'm awake now, but I can't stop shaking. I try to pray, but I keep thinking about how I could have stopped Thes's death. I can't talk to Heavenly Father any easier than I can talk to my parents. I miss Thes. I miss him so much. I need him.

Thes's name used to be Lautaro, the name of a Mapuche Indian. I want to tell him how I looked up the Mapuche tribe on the Internet last week. I want to tell him everything I found out about our heritage. And so I do. I talk to the darkness:

Thes, did you know that the Mapuches of Southern Chile were the only South American Indians to have successfully resisted conquest by the Spanish? They loved the earth more than gold. They believed that the world was held in precarious balance by two gods: Wefuku, the god of death and destruction, and Ngenechen, the positive god of love and creation. Then, when the Europeans came to South America, Wefuku threw his mantle of darkness over the world, overpowering Ngenechen, and throwing the earth out of balance.

That's how it feels now, Thes, like there is a blanket of shadow over everything. Remember when Mom wrote that poem titled "Balance"? She wrote it after a spring storm when flooding followed a winter of drought. It went something like this: Too fat, too thin, too much, too little, aching for balance we fall. What is the secret of spring storm, she asked in the last stanza. Then she answered her question. Perhaps we must learn to live well unbalanced. She can't do it though. Dad can't. I can't either. We can't. Your memory is like an empty space that weighs so much. You were too much a part of our worlds.

Remember eleven years ago when Dad took the training wheels off my bike? I was so scared. But he held the bike securely, reassuring me over and over again that he wouldn't let me fall. He would help me keep my balance. And I didn't fall. When he let go of the bike, I balanced on my own.

The day after I learned to ride my bike, Thes, you and I were in the driveway alone. "Show me how you can ride your bike," you said. It was more of a command than a suggestion.

"But Mom and Dad aren't here," I argued, "I can't ride without them."

"Chicken Little," you scoffed. Then you softened. "I'm here. I won't let you fall."

I gave in. You held the bike while I straddled it. I pressed my foot to the pedal, my heart pounding against my chest like horses' hooves. I started forward with you gripping the bike, holding me up. Then, you tripped over the curb and fell. The bike careened out of control. I landed with the bike on top of me. I cried while you worked to untangle the bike and me. "You let me fall down!" I sniffled.

Then, as you lifted the bike off of me, I saw that you were crying too. You never cried! Too surprised to cry anymore, I reached up and touched your damp cheek.

"Why are you crying?" I asked.

"It's my fault, little sister," you whispered. The sun and your tears made your cheeks shine. "I said I would hold you up." I wrapped my arms around you and hugged you. You hadn't cried when you got stitches. Did you really love me enough to cry for me?

Now, I'm the one crying, Thes. I just need to talk to you, to know for sure that you are still alive somewhere, even if it's in some other universe or dimension. I knelt down a minute ago. Even though I am guilty, I begged Heavenly Father to tell me you exist.

Then I crawled into my bed and tried to sleep, but the images from my dream returned. I struggled and freed myself from Mom's and Dad's grasp. Alone, each of us floated to the surface to breathe. Then, we searched for you, Thes, on the dark shore. But we couldn't find you and morning never came.

"Wake up!" Dennie opened her eyes to see the small hand of Christopher Parker shake her shoulder. She trembled as thoughts of the night before tumbled through her.

"Dennie!" The seven-year-old insisted now, shaking her mercilessly.

Dennie struggled to get her bearings. The blinds were open. Sunlight streamed in. The clock on her nightstand told her that it was 11:00 in the morning. She seemed to remember her mother coming in hours earlier, kissing her forehead as softly as the feel of butterfly wings, and opening the blinds. Was that when she had finally fallen into a deep, dreamless sleep? And here was Chris, with the slight sunburn on his upturned nose shaped like the drawing of a small vase, and his hair and smile full of the morning light. It was like a memory of happiness. Dennie swallowed. "Hey, Chris," she managed a smile. "How'd you get sunburned in the winter?"

"Blake took Mom and me skiing yesterday," Chris bounced on her bed. "Did you know we're going to be cousins?"

"No," Dennie said. "I did not know that. I absolutely did not know that."

Chris stopped bouncing and grinned. "My mom and your uncle are getting married. That means we are going to be cousins. That means we are going to play together. I'm going to bring a tent over and we'll set it up in the backyard and sleep in it. That's what cousins do."

"Really?" Dennie pulled her bathrobe on. Chris grabbed her hand and led her into the kitchen that smelled of hot chocolate and donuts. Blake, Karin, and Dennie's parents sat at the table eating and chatting. Her mom looked so together and calm, her hair neatly framing her face, her makeup on, her dark jeans and light-purple blouse pressed and clean. Dennie thought of how people have so many different places inside of them, like basement rooms hidden beneath a house. It hardly seemed possible that this was the same person who wept so jaggedly last night. The four adults turned to Dennie, greeting her cheerfully.

"Chris woke me up," Dennie smiled back. "I hear there's news."

"Why you little stinker!" Karin snorted. "I told you that Blake wanted to break the news to Dennie himself."

"So it's true," Dennie said enthusiastically as she looked at the happy couple. "Congratulations you guys!"

"Oh, Dennie, I'm so happy!" Karin exclaimed as she arose from the table and grabbed Dennie's hand. Karin's fingers were freckled and so warm and moist that they felt sticky. "Last night Blake asked me to marry him. He got down on his knees even. I—I said yes!" Dennie thought about how if Aimy were here she would have said how stupid people act when they are in love. But Dennie didn't think it was stupid. Yet, it felt as if it wasn't really happening, as if Dennie was caught inside herself, as if the people around her were actors on the screen of her vision saying their lines, enjoying their roles. And she, Dennie, was watching them from afar.

"Years ago I felt like I was trapped in a sort of prison. And now, with Blake, it feels like the sun will never stop shining!" Karin continued, beaming.

Chris piped in. "Mom, Joseph Smith was in prison too! He was in Liberty and Cartilage."

Laughter burst from the adults. "Son, I think you mean Carthage, not cartilage," Karin explained gently.

"But everyone has their own cartilage too," Blake said. "It's stuff that's not as hard as bones. Here and here." Blake wiggled Chris's nose and ears. Chris giggled.

Blake turned to Dennie and gave her a full hug. "Can you believe it, sweetie? Your Uncle Blake-o is getting hitched!" As she felt her uncle's heart beat and heard the laughter in the air, Dennie knew she was a part of the world again. She was glad her uncle had someone to love. "I'm happy for you, Uncle Blake," she said. "I'm very happy for both of you."

Then, as swiftly as rain can turn to snow, a wave of panic rose in Dennie. She was afraid of losing this wavering feeling of joy, this feeling of being a part of her family. "Hey, Chris," she yelled, "bring over the tent tonight! After I get back from the Kings game, we'll sleep out!" Christopher Parker let out an elated whoop. Blake and Karin hugged her once more like she was the greatest. Her parents looked at her with caution, as if they wondered who *this* Dennie was. "Are you sure, Dennie?" her father asked.

"Of course I'm sure. I always wanted a cousin to play with." She winked at Chris.

"We rode bikes over!" Chris shouted. "Come outside and ride

bikes with me, Dennie."

"I can't, Cuz. I work from twelve to four. But I'll see you tonight. I have to shower and get ready now." Dennie tousled his blond hair before leaving the room.

As she showered, Dennie closed her eyes. She pictured Chris's golden smile. She used it to push away the memory of her brother's tears.

CHAPTER 8

The Game

Aimy nervously eyed the clock. It was almost three and she was scheduled to work until eight. At least she was working the drive-through and there weren't any cars at the moment. Jerking her headphones off, she wheeled around to Dennie who was hefting a basket of fries out of a bin of hot grease.

"Den, will you work for me till eight tonight? My mom wasn't feeling well earlier and I need to go home and be with her."

Dennie wiped her brow. "I'm sorry, Aim, I can't. Remember, I'm going to the Kings game with the Babcocks. They're picking me up at ten after six."

"You get off at four, right?"

"Yeah."

"How about if you stay until six and work for me. I'll go home and check on Mom. Then, I'll be back. Call Ronny-boy and have him pick you up here." Aimy's voice was intense, demanding.

"Aimy, what's wrong with Moni?"

"A really bad stomach flu," Aimy lied. There were too many people around to tell Dennie the truth. "I'm worried she could get dehydrated or something."

"OK, I'll cover for you. The problem is that I don't have a change of clothes here. I can't go to the game dressed like a farmhand. Maybe you could stop by my house and bring me back some clothes."

Aimy hugged Dennie. "Thanks, Density. I owe you one. I told you Ronny-boy was going to ask you out."

"It's not really a date. It's like a family thing. Bring back my black jeans, my blue sweater, and my makeup bag."

Outside, a van pulled up to the drive-through menu. The driver honked the horn impatiently. "Aimy, get back to your station!" Sean Miller boomed good-naturedly.

"Would you take this one for me, Sean-ee? I've gotta make some phone calls."

"Sure thing, Babe," Sean strode over and grabbed the headphones. Aimy blew him a kiss.

"Aim," Dennie said as she shoveled fries into baskets, "call my parents and tell them not to pick me up at four. Make sure my mom understands that I'm going straight to the game. She's been paranoid lately. I'll call Babcocks later and tell them to pick me up here."

Aimy went into Owen's office to use the telephone. She was glad he was in Hawaii for three weeks. He disgusted her. It got old, feigning friendliness.

But where was her mom? Earlier that morning, Moni had left for work—at least that was where Aimy thought she was going. Then, an hour later, Raylene from the Gemini Store had called and asked for Moni. "Why's she late?" There had been an edge in Raylene's voice. "Moni's client's waiting." Aimy had lied, telling Raylene that her mom was up all night with the stomach flu. Aimy had apologized profusely, extending the story by explaining that Moni was sleeping now and Aimy had forgotten to awaken her. She had even shouldered the blame, saying that it was her own fault that Moni hadn't called in sick. Aimy didn't enjoy lying, but it seemed a necessity for survival. Moni couldn't afford to lose her job. Where was her mother?

Aimy tossed her head in order to shake aside the fear. She focused on the moment at hand and picked up the telephone. She called the Fletchers first. Meryl answered and Aimy relayed Dennie's message. Before hanging up, Mrs. Fletcher chatted with Aimy about Blake and Karin's engagement. She mentioned that Chris had made plans to spend the night in the tent with Dennie. "Aimy, why don't you come over too and keep Dennie company," Meryl offered. "There's plenty of room in the tent and we have an extra sleeping bag. Just dress really warm."

After saying good-bye and hanging up, Aimy thought about how lucky Dennie was in some ways. She had a great mom. No matter how hard things were, Dennie was taken care of. She would be all right. Then, Aimy dialed her own number. It rang four times. She heard the sound of her own voice on the answering machine. She waited for the beep. "Pick up, Mom! Pick up!" Aimy called into the phone. Nothing. Aimy slammed down the receiver. Even when Moni was home, she often turned off the phone. For an instant Aimy felt like she might throw up. She went into the bathroom, splashed water on her face, and went back out to work.

When Aimy came back to the drive-through window, Sean refused to give up his seat.

"Get out of here," he barked.

"You're stealing my seat! I'm scheduled to work drive-through today," Aimy argued as she struggled to wrestle the headphones from him.

"But I'm assistant manager. This isn't a democracy. And possession is nine tenths of the law," he laughed. "Go clean tables."

"Over my dead body!" Aimy attempted to pull the swivel chair out from under him. Then, a car pulled up. Sean peacefully relinquished the station. But as Aimy put the earphones on, he slipped a handful of ice down her back. She squirmed and shot him an *I'll get you back for this* look. Yet, even as she shook the ice from her overalls, her voice was smooth as a summer day while she spoke to the customer in the car. "Hi! May I help you?"

After she finished the order, Sean came over and took the earphones off her head. "Get out of here," he said and his voice was gentle. "Go check on your mom."

Aimy decided to check at home first. When she arrived, she found her mother sitting limply on the sofa with a drink next to her. Aimy forced herself to breathe normally. She would never let her mother know how relieved she felt. Moni's long, streaked blond hair lay plastered against her temples.

"Mom, where were you? Why didn't you answer the telephone?"

"I went over to Wayne's this morning. My head was pounding and he gave me some medicine. I was asleep when the telephone rang. Couldn't get to it in time." Moni's words slurred together.

"Raylene called! I told her you were sick."

"Thanks, Baby, I'm sorry." Moni didn't meet her daughter's eyes. "My head hurt so bad this morning. I had to take something."

"What did you take?" Aimy asked.

Moni skirted the question. "Baby, I don't know how things get so mixed up. Sometimes I just want to disappear."

"Mom, if we don't pay our bills we won't have electricity. We'll be on the street! I can't call Aunt Joni and ask for more money this month!" Aimy screamed as hot tears burned her eyes like flames.

"Honey," Moni said thickly. "I'll make it up to you. Tomorrow morning I'll get up and go to church with you. You look so cute in that farmhand outfit."

"Mom, you need professional help. You need to stop drinking, to stop taking so many pills."

"If I told the authorities, they'd take you away from me, put you into some foster home, and force me into rehab. I grew up in foster homes. It wasn't fun, never belonging. That's why I have to take stuff. So I'll feel better. So I can take care of you. So we can keep going. You're my baby and I'm your mommy. We're family."

Aimy took a deep breath and wiped her tears on the sleeve of her Beef Burger shirt. Then, Aimy called the Gemini Store and explained to Raylene that Moni was feeling better and would be back to work on Monday. She swept the floor, cleaned the kitchen, made the bed, scrubbed the bathroom, and cooked Moni a dinner of scrambled eggs and toast. When the phone rang, she didn't answer it. Aimy left the house at 6:00. At 6:10, she pulled into the Beef Burgers parking lot. Dennie waited outside. Aimy realized that she had forgotten to pick up her friend's clothes.

"Is your mom OK?" Dennie asked.

"Not right now. She'll be OK tomorrow. It's just a twenty-four-hour thing. She even promised to go to church with me. That would be a surprise!"

Dennie studied her friend. "Aim, where's my stuff?"

Aimy thumped her head with the heel of her hand. "Density, I forgot it! Can you believe it! I guess I'm the dense one! I'm so sorry! I was just cleaning up after my mom and it slipped my mind."

"What am I going to do?" Dennie asked as the Babcock's van pulled into the parking lot.

"I don't know. Leave your coat on. Ask the Babcocks to stop by your house on the way. It'll take ten minutes. What's ten minutes? I owe you big time, Density. I'll come over tonight and help you baby-sit Chris."

Dennie felt her face redden in frustration. The van pulled up. Everyone inside waved and called "hellos" to Aimy. The bishop was driving and Tammy sat perched in the front passenger's seat. Dennie climbed in, said a brief good-bye to Aimy and sat down in the back next to Ron.

"Hey, Dennie," Ron grinned. "Fasten your seatbelt. My dad is driving."

"My dad had to go to traffic school last month," Tammy chirped. The van grazed the curb as they pulled out of the parking lot.

"Dennie, don't listen to them." The bishop pushed his glasses up with one hand and steered with the other. "You used to be able to do U-turns on Grantlin Boulevard. I didn't know that had changed."

"It changed two years ago, Dad," Ron laughed. "And what about the parked car you backed into? How do you explain that?"

The bishop was in the middle of a lengthy explanation when Ron interrupted. "Dad! The car ahead has its brake lights on. Slow down!" The bishop jammed on the brakes while Dennie clutched the armrest.

"Bishop," Dennie said when they were safely stopped at the light. "Would it be possible to turn around? I need to stop by my house. I didn't get a chance to change."

"Sure, Dennie." Bishop Babcock pivoted his head and tossed her a smile. "There's plenty of time." Then, when the light turned green, he swung the van across the turning lane and did a U-turn so that they would be going the right direction on Grantlin Boulevard.

"Daddy," Tammy chimed, "it isn't legal to do U-turns on Grantlin Boulevard anymore."

When they pulled up to the Fletcher's home, Dennie didn't notice the sedan with the tinted windows parked close by. Perhaps it was because Ron sat so close to her that his warmth distracted her, or maybe it was the silly joke the bishop had just told.

Whatever the reason, she was already in the house and halfway through the kitchen when she saw Ty Edwards standing at the counter, chopping vegetables with her mother. The two chatted amicably, like they had done this before, like they were mother and son. Dennie gasped audibly and stopped short. They turned towards her, their eyes wide in surprise.

"Dennie," her mom was the first to find her voice. "Dad and I were lonely without you tonight, so we invited Ty over for dinner. Is everything OK?"

"The Babcocks are waiting. Aimy forgot to get my clothes. I've gotta change," Dennie's sentences were short, like bullets.

"You're going to love watching Jason Williams," Ty said like nothing was wrong, like he belonged here. "That guy has the moves."

Dennie's mother turned to get some vegetables from the fridge. While her mother's back was turned, Dennie fled to her bedroom. She changed her clothes, her heart pounding the wall of her chest like a battering ram.

Bishop Gary Babcock could tell that Dennie Fletcher wasn't focused on the game. She didn't see the magic of Jason William's wrap-around-the-back, make-the-ball-disappear dribble. She didn't laugh at the antics of Slamson, the Kings' lion mascot, or become enraged when four fouls were called on Big Nasty Chris Webber, before half time. Sure she clapped when Ron clapped. Sure she made herself smile. But the bishop could tell the difference. Something had happened before the game, at the Fletcher's home. When she came back out to the car, her face was red, her laughter too loud. When the bishop looked at her in the rearview mirror, her eyes were blank and distracted. He had noticed Ty Edward's car at the house. Ty was the young man Theseus had saved. The bishop recalled speaking at the boy's funeral; he had compared Thes's love for Ty to the Savior's charity. Did Dennie blame Ty for the loss of her brother's life? Dennie Fletcher was one of Bishop Babcock's youth, part of his flock. Bishop Gary Babcock was determined to help her through this.

During half-time, while Dennie took Tammy to the bathroom, the bishop decided to share his thoughts with his son, Ron. "Be her friend, Ron," he said. "Her parents have told me that she doesn't seem herself. They can't reach her right now. Maybe you can."

"There's nothing I'd like better than to reach Dennie," Ron said. The bishop chuckled and put his hand on his son's knee. Dennie and Tammy returned. On the floor of Arco arena the Royal Court Dancers shimmied.

"Dennie," Tammy whispered. "My brother thinks you are prettier than the Royal Court girls. He says you have eyes like Bambi's." Dennie felt her cheeks turn red, but this time it wasn't from anger.

CHAPTER 9

Strength of Will

After the game, Ron talked his father into letting him drive home. Ron knew he was a decent driver even though he had only had his license a couple of months. Yet, tonight it was hard to focus on the road. He felt intensely aware of Dennie Fletcher in the passenger seat next to him. He couldn't stop himself from looking over from time to time and glimpsing her profile. He noticed the curve of her eyelashes, the shape of the space between her nose and lips. She sat so still she hardly seemed to be breathing. He wondered what she was thinking about and what she thought about him. He heard his little sister's deep rhythmical breathing in the back seat. That kid could sleep anywhere. He adjusted the rearview mirror and saw Tammy, snoring now, with her head bent at an awkward angle against his father's shoulder. Ron thought about how the Kings had won. Now their spot in the playoffs was secure. He would have been completely happy if only he dared reach out and hold Dennie's hand.

When they neared the Grantlin exit, Bishop Babcock spoke, "Dennie, do you mind if Ron drops Tammy and me off first? I want to get this kid to bed."

"That's fine," Dennie said. Her voice sounded so even and calm. Yet Ron felt as if his body was full of electricity. After he dropped his dad and sister off, he couldn't stop his thumb from thumping the steering wheel, or his heel from bouncing up and down.

A few minutes later, Ron pulled the van into the Fletcher's driveway. He walked Dennie to the front door. "I hope you had fun," he said, shuffling his feet, feeling more than just a year younger than this lovely girl whose black silk eyes made him light-headed. He was nearly certain that she didn't take him seriously. Why had he taken his dad and sister on their first date? He thought of how his face was freckled and broken out, while her warm complexion was smooth as satin. These thoughts made him feel clumsy and dorkish. And, at that moment, the last thing on earth Ron Babcock wanted to be was a dork.

"It was a great game," Dennie commented with a slight smile. Ron remembered how, during the final quarter, the Kings had made a run and pulled ahead. Ron had exploded into cheers, forgetting all clumsiness and draping his arm around Dennie's shoulder and squeezing her tight. At that moment, he had felt his enthusiasm reach her. She had finally sensed the electric energy of the crowd, the thrill of the game, the joy of victory. Her cheers had become dynamic. The memory lent Ron courage.

"I hear Brother Blake-o's guitar," Ron said. Strains of Blake singing *You are my lady and I am your man* seeped from the house.

"He's serenading Karin Parker. They're waiting with Chris until I get home," Dennie explained. "Did I tell you that I promised to camp out in the tent with Chris tonight?"

"What the heck?" Ron burst. "It's winter time! *You* are going to freeze!"

Dennie giggled at Ron's shocked tone and tossed her head. He noticed her hair ripple down her back. Dennie added, "Chris wants to because we're going to be cousins. He's so cute. He told me that's what cousins do."

"You are an insane woman," Ron said. "You need to learn to say no to crazy little kids. Be assertive! I've had lots of practice with Tammy. I could lend her to you!"

"It wouldn't help. I've never been very assertive," Dennie said quietly. Ron saw a shadow cross her features. Almost like she had been hit by a wave of pain.

"Dennie, are you OK?" Ron asked.

"Uh-huh."

"Sometimes you get this look in your eyes. Like you're really sad or on another planet or something."

Dennie smiled. Ron noticed that it didn't reach her eyes. She spoke, "Ron, I was just thinking about what you said. I need to be more assertive. Not with Chris, I'm OK with that. But in other ways."

"What other ways?"

Dennie sighed. It was quiet for a moment.

"Well, you need some practice." Ron broke the silence. He was going to make her laugh again tonight if it was the last thing he did on earth.

"At what?"

"At being strong-willed. At saying *no*." Ron grabbed a twig off the ground and pretended like he was smoking. "Baby," he said, putting his arm around her and pulling her into him. He pretended like he was breathing smoke down her neck. "Baby, have a draw."

"Uh, no." Dennie shook away from him and rewarded him with a small smile. That was closer. Ron would draw a laugh from her yet.

"Excellenté! Now we'll try a different scenario inspired by Brother Blake-o and Sister Parker!" Ron dropped to his knees on the sidewalk and took her hand in both of his. He sang dramatically. "You are my woman, and I am your fink. Marry me in Vegas. Who cares if I stink!"

Dennie's face spread into a grin. She sang back softly. "I am a woman and you are a guppy. Get out of my life before I throw uppy!"

"A+!" Ron laughed and jumped to his feet. "See, you can do it!"

When Ron began talking again, he spoke quickly, catching his breath off and on, like he couldn't quite organize his thoughts. "Next week, Glenn Allen . . . Do you know him? He's Sister Allen's husband and Mike Carlo's stepfather. Anyway, he's bringing home some mustangs. Not cars, horses. Last year he got interested in wild horses. He wants to help save them. It's Presidents' Day so Elise and Mike are coming home from college to see the mustangs. Actually, I think it's an excuse to see each other. Anyway do you want to go out there and see the horses, and watch Glenn work with them?"

"No, thank you," Dennie said.

Ron's face fell, but an instant later he managed a smile which looked like it had had been wrenched into place by a pair of pliers. "Hey, that's OK. Shoot, you probably don't like horses, or you have other plans or something."

Dennie giggled and her eyes laughed. "I'm just kidding, Ron. I'm practicing saying *no* like you suggested. I'd really like to go."

"Great," Ron laughed too. Yet, he found it uncomfortable switching from despair to joy in no more time than it takes for a breath of air.

Twenty minutes later Dennie was in the tent with Chris. She wore woolen socks, long underwear, a pair of black sweats, and two sweatshirts in contrast with Chris's light-cotton Star Wars pajamas. Karin crawled into the tent and kissed Chris goodnight.

"Is Chris dressed warmly enough?" Dennie asked when Karin was on her way out.

"The child has no nerves! He doesn't feel cold!" Karin laughed.

After Blake and Karin drove away, Dennie and Chris crawled into their sleeping bags. Dennie watched her breath swirl in the cold air. Ron was right! She was going to freeze! Yet, if Chris fell asleep quickly, she could sneak into the house, spend the night in her own bed, then hustle back to the tent early the next morning before he awakened.

The problem was that Chris talked incessantly. He was a million miles away from sleep. No wonder he doesn't feel the cold, Dennie thought; his little mouth burns enough energy to keep his entire body warm! Dennie, on the other hand, felt tiredness engulf her. She longed to close her eyes.

"Did you know there are lots of different kinds of goldfish?" Chris asked as he shined the flashlight into her eyes. Dennie blinked uncontrollably. Chris continued. His voice rang with excitement. "There's the Common Goldfish like you get at the fair. But there are other kinds too, like the Fantail, the Orandu, and the Ryunkin." He was quiet for a moment and Dennie dozed. Then, the flashlight blazed against her eyelids, startling her like the brightness of the second coming. She threw her arm up. Chris continued, "I'm going to use goldfish in my science project. Mom says I can buy two of each kind. Then I'm going to put them in bowls with their own seashells. Seashells are like toys to them. Then, after a few days I'm going to build a maze. I'm going to see if the goldfish can find their own seashells. I'm also going to see which kind is fastest."

"Wow," Dennie managed, wondering if it would be cousinly to grab the flashlight from Chris and knock him out with it. Suddenly there were two thuds in the backyard, followed by heavy breathing.

"Dennie!" Chris screamed, bolting out of his sleeping bag and into Dennie's arms. He dropped his flashlight. It balanced on the sleeping bag, shining on his pajamas, causing the image of Darth Vader to wobble as he trembled. There were footsteps in the yard.

"Sh," Dennie whispered, "It could be Darth Vader in the flesh!"

"In da flesh! In da flesh!!" answered Aimy's slithering voice from outside the tent.

"I want my mommy!" Chris screamed. He felt bony in Dennie's arms. She felt his heart beat against her, quickly, like a bird's. She suddenly felt mean. "It's OK," she whispered. "It's just my friend, Aimy, trying to scare us."

A moment later, Aimy unzipped the tent door and crawled in with her sleeping bag and flashlight in tow.

"Just thought I'd join *all y'all.*"

"Who's *all y'all?*" Chris asked as he eyed her suspiciously.

"You and your cuz, Dennie. You see, in the deep south *y'all* only refers to one person. If you're talking to more than one person you have to say *all y'all.*"

"No way!" Chris rejoined.

"Yes way! Just ask Sean Garrett. He just came back from a mission in South Carolina. Tonight, he said, 'Aimy, y'all come over here and give me a hand with these French fries.' I said, 'I'm just one person, not *y'all.*' He said, 'If I wanted more than one person I would have said, *All y'all* come over here and give me a hand with these fries!'"

Chris giggled. "OK, you can stay!" he announced. "But y'all have to sleep on the other side of me, not by Dennie. She's my cousin."

"A bit possessive, aren't we," Aimy said as she spread out her sleeping bag. "Now, Chris, it's time to play the quiet game," Aimy announced as she took the flashlight from him and hung both flashlights from the pole at the top of the tent. "It's the humans against the flashlights. Whoever makes the first move or the first sound loses."

To Dennie's utter amazement, Chris froze. She and Aimy joined him, swallowing giggles as they glued their eyes on the flashlights. After ten minutes of silence, Chris was fast asleep.

"Aim, you are brilliant." Dennie said when he was breathing evenly. "I couldn't get that little boy to shut up. Thanks for coming."

Aimy laughed and stood up to retrieve the flashlights. She handed one to Dennie. She crawled back into her sleeping bag and they both turned off the lights.

"Den, did you have fun tonight?"

"Yeah," Dennie said. "Ron is really nice."

"How do you feel about him?"

"I don't know."

"Density, you are so weird. Whenever I'm with a guy I know exactly how I feel about him."

"I mean I've never thought about Ron in *that* way before. I've always thought of him as a funny guy, a nice person, straight as an arrow, the bishop's kid."

Aimy's next comment surprised Dennie. "I wonder if someone like that could ever like me. A funny guy, straight as an arrow. That's the kind of guy I want to marry."

"Aimy, do you *like* Ron?" Dennie asked, astounded.

"No, no, no! Density, I mean someone with those qualities. Not Ronny-boy. Ronny-boy is way too boyish for me."

Dennie was quiet for a moment. She remembered Ron's arm around her at the game; the feel of his hands clasping hers on the porch when they laughed. *Boyish* didn't seem like such a bad thing.

Aimy began talking again. "When I met with Bishop Babcock last Sunday, he told me that I needed to quit going out with Brak for my own physical and spiritual safety. He even helped me write a letter to Brak telling him never to come near me again."

"A very wise man," Dennie said.

Aimy pulled an envelope out of her pocket. It was folded and wrinkled, but it had a stamp on it and Brak's name and address. "Den, will you mail it for me?"

"Sure." Dennie reached over Chris and took the envelope from Aimy.

"Thanks," Aimy said. Her voice sounded old and tired.

"How's your mom feeling?" Dennie changed the subject.

"She's OK. I came over here after she fell asleep. She didn't really have the flu. She'd been drinking and missed work again today. I'm sorry about forgetting your clothes."

"It's OK. The Babcocks took me home to change. Ty Edwards was there with my parents. Why doesn't he just stay away?"

"Dennie, Ty didn't want Thes to die. Maybe he's trying to make up for it."

For a few moments silence filled the tent. "Aim," Dennie began. "When Brak told you how Thes died, how did he know? Did Ty tell him?"

Aimy remembered the day, a month after the funeral, when Brak had yanked her from her locker and had told her that Ty had lied, that he, Brak, had witnessed Thes's death, that the death had been a drunken accident. But Aimy had thought Brak was the one lying, trying to hurt her for breaking up with him, for caring about Thes. Yet, even in her rage, she had felt the strange chemistry between them, like Brak was a magnet and she couldn't escape his pull. Later that day, she had started to tell Dennie shreds of the story. "Don't talk about it anymore!" Dennie had begged and Dennie's face had turned the slate gray of the sky. Aimy had never mentioned it again. She had decided that it didn't matter what the truth was. It only mattered that Thes was dead. But, now, in the dark of the tent, blanketed by her sleeping bag, she knew Dennie needed to hear exactly what Brak had said.

"Brak told me that he followed Ty and Thes that day. You know how the windows on Ty's car are tinted. Brak wanted to know if I was in the backseat or if I was going to meet Thes somewhere. You know how Brak is, crazy jealous. That's why I have to stay away from him. Brak supposedly followed them all the way to the ocean, staying back far enough so they didn't know he was there. Then, he parked along the highway. He looked down the bluffs and could see the rocks where Thes and Ty were fishing. He said that he saw Thes drinking and stumbling around. He said Thes acted like he didn't even care that the water was rough. He was too drunk. A wave took him. Ty went in after him, but it was too late. It might not be true, Den. Brak is capable of lying."

Dennie didn't answer. Aimy reached over Chris and took hold of Dennie's hand. They slept with their fingers tightly entwined, their arms forming a rope over the sleeping child.

When Dennie awakened the next morning, Aimy was gone. Chris was still asleep. Dennie reached under her pillow and felt the letter to Brak, the crisp, dry paper in her hand. She looked at Chris. His eyelids fluttered, reminding Dennie of the quick shudder of a bird's wing.

CHAPTER 10

Whatever Will Be

About six months after we came to the United States, Mom took us to a pediatrician for a checkup. He said that I looked about five years old, but intellectually I seemed older than that, at least six. Thes was most likely seven or eight years old. He was definitely older than his sister (doctors are brilliant sometimes), but not more than nine. The doctor was sorry he couldn't be more exact. But everything was approximate, nothing for sure.

"But when's my birthday?" Thes asked.

"Mine too?" I echoed.

The doctor shook his head. "I don't know."

"Hey!" Mom grinned as our expressions drooped. "We can pick your birthdays! How many families get to do that!"

We decided on March 21 for Thes, the spring equinox, the day the Greek Theseus entered the labyrinth and defeated the minataur, a monster with the body of a man and the head of a bull. My birthday would be six months later, September 21, the first day of fall, the autumnal equinox. The dictionary defines equinox as the time when the sun crosses the celestial equator. It is the time when seasons change and day and night are equal, when light and darkness balance. Once Dad mentioned that a severe storm often occurs during or near the time of equinox.

We had been in the United States about a year when September 21 came. Two big events occurred that day. One was the celebration of my approximate six years of life. The other was our family's sealing in the Oakland temple. I remember Grandma Elsa Hudsfeldt Fletcher, Daddy's mom, arriving at our house early that morning. I loved her German accent, her round blue-gray eyes surrounded by spider webs of fine wrinkles, and her silver hair sprayed into firm waves shaped something like half-moons.

Grandma Elsa came laden with two packages wrapped in golden ribbon. She said that the gifts were for us both because it was more than just my birthday. It was a day of eternal beginnings. The first package was filled with a white dress for me and a white shirt and white knickers for Thes. She had made them for us to wear in the temple. My dress was intricately lovely with hand-embroidered lace and delicate smocking. I held it up against me and twirled.

I opened the second package. It contained two thick books. One was a collection of Grimm's fairy tales and the other a book of Bible stories. "Just books!" Thes moaned. I took the Bible storybook and began leafing through it.

"What do you mean 'just books?'" Grandma Elsa's resonant voice pinned Thes like a wrestler's hold. "These are beautiful books, hardbound and expensive. Just look at the artwork in them. Look at the golden edges and the silk ribbons to mark your place. I wrote you and your sister a note in these books. These books will be around long after I'm gone. You come right over here to the sofa and sit by me, Thes. I'll read you a story and we'll see whether or not you like these books." While Mom put our clothes in the van, I overheard Grandma Elsa reading Thes the story of Hansel and Grettel.

A little while later we piled into the car for the long drive to the temple. We picked up Uncle Blake on the way. I slept off and on with grown-up talk floating around me. I awoke when the car reached the top of a hill and there it was—white, with high spires and carvings of Jesus and his disciples! There was a waterfall. Dad parked and we got out. The sun shone. Thes and I ran to the edge of the hill. We looked down and saw the city below dimmed and softened by blue-gray fog.

"Mina, you could fall down into that city if you aren't careful. You have to be careful," Thes whispered to me. He hadn't called me 'Mina' for months. "I won't," I answered. "I'll be careful."

When we went inside the temple, a worker dressed in white tried to whisk Thes and me away to the nursery. She said that she would help us to dress and bring us to the sealing room when it was time. But Grandma Elsa balked. "I'm going to the nursery with these children. They need their grandmother. You don't want them frightened, do you?"

In the nursery, we watched a movie about eternal families. Then, Grandma and Thes built jets with legos until it was time to dress. After we put on our white clothes, Grandma stroked our black hair with a soft brush until it shone. "You are ready now!" she declared, beaming.

Thes and I held hands when we walked into the sealing room. There were about thirty people staring at us. I recognized some of them from church. I heard muffled gasps and whispers of "what beautiful children." But it was the room that was beautiful to me. I still see it in my mind. Chandeliers as bright and clean as joy, walls white as hope, and mirrors facing each other, their reflections going on and on.

In the center of the room, there was a velvet altar blanketed by lace. I remember kneeling at the altar with my parents. Mommy smiled at me with eyes like a bright blue sky full of star-like tears. After the ceremony, the kind man, the temple sealer, told us to stand together as a family and look into the mirrors at our images going on forever. We were now a celestial family.

In the car, on the way back home, Thes leaned against Grandma and asked her to read him the story of Hansel and Grettel once more. He loved the part where Hansel dropped the white stones that shone like silver coins in the moonlight, the stones that later led Hansel and Grettel back home. He was interested in the white bird that guided the children to the cottage in the woods, then came back again as a snowy duck to carry Hansel and Grettel across the lake to the part of the forest they knew. He said the stepmother was much worse than the wicked witch because even though the witch was going to eat the children, at least she fed them too. He said that Hansel was smart like a boy and Grettel was scared like a girl. "But Grettel saved Hansel in the end," Grandma Elsa reminded him as she winked wickedly at me.

Thes changed the subject. "God sent the white birds to help the children," he told us.

"How do you know that?" Grandma Elsa asked. "It doesn't say that in the story."

"I know!" Thes said.

"Heavenly Father does things like that. He sent a white bird when Jesus was baptized," I mentioned.

"And Noah sent a white dove from the ark to see if the rain was gone," Uncle Blake added.

"See!" Thes eyed Grandma.

"You're probably right," Grandma said. "You are a very smart boy."

I took the book from Grandma and looked at the pictures. I looked at the words. I knew the letters well enough to read the story myself. "When Grettel shook out her apron," I read out loud, "the pearls and jewels bounced about the room. Hansel added to the joy by throwing one handful after another from his pocket. Now, all their problems were finished and they lived with their father happily ever after."

"Did you know she could read like that?" Grandma asked Mom. Mom nodded her head slightly.

"It doesn't surprise me," Uncle Blake said. Grandma Elsa winked at me again. "These two are very smart children," she said like it was an announcement. "They are very smart children." It was September twenty-first when the hours of day equaled the hours of night, just before the coming day when darkness would outweigh light.

Dennie held the letter that Aimy had asked her to mail to Brak above the mouth of the mailbox. It was light and would easily sail to its recipient on one postage stamp. She was about to toss it in when a chill went through her. She was afraid of Brak's reaction. He was so unpredictable. Why hadn't Aimy mailed it herself? Why had Aimy made Dennie responsible?

For some unknown reason she remembered a moment years ago at Splash World. She was twelve years old and had climbed with Thes and Aimy to the top of a tubular waterslide called The Snake. Thes went down first. Then it was Dennie's turn. She positioned herself at the top but was afraid to let go. She closed her eyes and asked Aimy to push her. Aimy did. Dennie's arms jerked upwards as she fell into darkness. She felt the whoosh of water around her. She felt like she was being flushed down a toilet. Then there was light and she landed in a pool. Seconds later, Aimy was next to her and they were laughing. Dennie remembered jumping up and down in the water, giddy with the joy of courage and friendship.

"Excuse me, are you going to mail that letter? I hate to intrude, but I have a bundle that needs to get out and I'm in a bit of a hurry. I have an appointment in five minutes." A short grandmotherish woman approached Dennie with a stack of rubber-banded letters in her hands.

"Oh, sorry," Dennie said as she let the letter slide from her fingers into the mailbox.

"It must be important," the woman commented as she mailed her bundle. "I could tell by the way you were thinking about it and waiting."

"It was important," Dennie said.

The woman grinned knowingly at Dennie. "I'll bet it was to a boy."

Dennie smiled falsely and nodded. Sometimes it was easier to let people think what they wanted to think, to imagine whatever was in their imagination.

"Well, I'd say he was one lucky boy. Don't look so worried, dear. It's on its way now. Whatever will be will be. The future's not ours to see."

CHAPTER 11

Me Too, You

It was the Saturday before I started fourth grade and Thes started fifth. Even though the afternoon was hot enough to melt feet into pavement, Thes and I decided to ride our bikes to our school, Alta Elementary, to find out which teachers we would have. As I pedaled vigorously down the bike trail, trying to keep up with my brother, I prayed that I wouldn't get Mrs. Spinelly. She was nicknamed the spider due to her huge stomach, thin legs and poisonous tongue. When Thes had her the year before, she told the class that she sucked the blood of children who forgot to do their homework.

My hair was pulled back into a tight ponytail. I felt drops of perspiration run down my temple. When I arrived at the school, Thes was already looking at the fifth-grade lists. I jerked my bike over the curb, past the parking lot, to the bike rack. I dismounted, pulling my sweat-sticky hands off the handlebar grips.

I felt like I was melting as I walked over to the office door where the class lists were posted. A girl whom I had never seen before stood in front of the fourth-grade lists. She ran her finger down the paper, searching for her name, totally oblivious to my presence. I stared at the back of her wrinkled T-shirt. Strings of waist-long, white-blond hair trickled down her neck. I cleared my throat, hoping she would notice me and make room.

Thes ambled over to me. "Are you ready to go, Dennie? I'm hot."

"We can't go yet," I said quietly. "I don't know who my teacher is."

The girl turned around, her washed-out blue eyes drinking us in. Her small bow-shaped mouth tilted into a smile. She had a pointed chin and reminded me of an elf.

"Hi," she said. "I'm Aimy. I'm new. What do you guys know about Spinelly?"

"She's the spider," Thes answered. "She lurks in corners and has poisonous fangs."

My eyes darted through the lists. There it was—FLETCHER, DENIZ after FLEMING, AARON.

"I have Spinelly too," I moaned. I felt like crying.

"Deniz, the menace! The spider's gonna suck your blood," Thes teased.

"Your name's Deniz, like a boy's. That's cool," Aimy peered at my name.

"Actually, it's Denizen, Dennie for short. They only print the first five letters on these stupid lists."

"Spider bait. You two are spider bait," Thes sighed dramatically.

"I know how to handle spiders!" Aimy turned her eyes towards Thes.

"Yeah, how?" Thes asked with a sideways smirk.

"She's a teacher. Use a Webster."

"A Webster?" Thes's voice dripped sarcasm. "One of those broom-like things mothers use to knock down webs. Yeah, sure."

Aimy replied, "Not that kind of Webster. She's a teacher so use a Webster Dictionary. It's a joke."

"Ha. Ha." Thes smirked but his eyes twinkled. I could tell that he thought Aimy was cool.

"I love your name, Dennie," Aimy said. "I love your eyes too. And your hair. I'm glad we're in the same class."

We talked for a few minutes. I found out that Aimy had attended Williams Elementary the year before. She would be moving in a couple of weeks and that would put her in the Alta Elementary boundaries. A worn truck pulled into the parking lot.

"Aimy, honey, let's go!" A woman called from inside the cab.

"Wait a sec, Moni! I made some friends!" Aimy yelled back.

"Girl, get your butt over here!" A man in the truck barked.

The woman said something to the man. Then, she got out of the truck and walked toward Aimy. She was attractive in a sexy sort of way with bleached, dark-rooted hair, like lemon-pepper seasoning. She had a short waist and high hips. She wore skimpy denim shorts that showed off her leggy tan. Her white tank top was tucked in. The lettering on it said, "Don't blame me, I voted for Elvis."

"Baby, introduce me to your friends," the woman said to Aimy.

"This is Dennie," Aimy replied.

"Dennie who?" she asked.

"Fletcher," I helped.

"And you?" She turned her eyes towards Thes.

"I'm Thes, her brother," Thes said coolly.

"Cool names for cool kids," Moni smiled at us. I noticed that some of Moni's teeth were gray. "Dennie and Thes, where do you live?"

I told her our address. Moni's green eyes flashed like sparklers. "I can't believe it! We're renting the house across the street! We move in next week. This was meant to be!"

"Mone, would you hurry it up!" the man yelled.

"Tell your friends good-bye," Moni said to Aimy as she turned and walked quickly to the truck.

"My mom," Aimy whispered like it explained everything.

"Is that your dad?" Thes asked.

"My new stepdad," Aimy gazed at the car. "A.k.a—the tarantula."

"It was nice meeting you," I called as Aimy broke into a run.

"See ya, Aimy," Thes waved.

"Me too, you!" Aimy grinned and yelled back to us both. As Thes and I walked to our bikes I watched Aimy climb into the cab. Her mother scooted over to sit in the middle of the bench seat next to her husband. There was a tiny hole in the passenger side of the windshield. Long crack lines radiated from the hole like twisted spokes or spider's legs. These cracks cut apart my view of Aimy and Moni, splitting their faces into sections, like pieces of a puzzle.

On Thursday, during Honors English, Ms. Harris pointed a long finger, with nails painted like watermelons, at Dennie. "Dennie Fletcher, you should have finished reading *The Heart of Darkness* last night. Review with the class Kurtz's final words and discuss why Marlow chose to lie to Kurtz's fiancée."

Ms. Harris's black hair flared out in all directions like dark flames, and her brown, bulging eyes held Dennie hostage. She was executioner and Dennie was victim. Dennie looked down, feeling as if she were putting her head on the block, ready for the guillotine. "I was working last night. I'm behind on my reading," she admitted.

"Do you work tonight?" Harris asked.

"No," Dennie said. "I'll catch up tonight."

"Come to my room after school and catch up in here with me," Ms. Harris said. Dennie nodded. Never before in her life had she faced detention. She felt her cheeks grow scarlet. She knew that some classmates were inwardly snickering, while others looked at her with compassion. She wished she could evaporate.

Harris paced through the room. "Would anyone else like to tackle this question?" Jeff Bridges, a guy with a long, narrow nose raised his hand. She pointed at him. "Kurtz's final words were 'The horror! The horror!' But Marlow tells Kurtz's girlfriend that his dying words were her name. How romantic!"

"What horror do you think Kurtz was referring to."

"Maybe he thought dying was terrible. Or maybe he hated his life. I don't know."

Ty Edwards raised his hand. "Maybe he was talking about himself. Kurtz, who was supposed to be some type of emissary of light, became like a heathen. He had all those skulls around his house. Maybe, at the end, he realized how evil he was. But it was too late."

"Yes, Ty! Outstanding!" Ms. Harris clapped her hands and did a tap dance in the aisle. "What Joseph Conrad is trying to tell us in this novel is that each human being has the capacity for evil. Often it is hidden like snags in a river, but it is there. I believe that. Yet, I also believe that each human being has an incredible capacity for good, the ability to add something positive to their world. Ty, why do you think Marlow lied to Kurtz's intended?"

"To protect her. To save her from being hurt."

"Perhaps," Harris went on. "Yet, Marlow considers the sea as inscrutable as destiny. It is mysterious. It hides reality. Do you think Marlow was justified in hiding reality from Kurtz's intended? Ty, is a lie ever justified?"

Dennie saw Ty's eyes cut to her, then away. His cheeks reddened and his Adam's apple convulsed as he swallowed.

"I don't know," Ty said quietly.

Heidi Crane raised her hand. "I think sometimes lies are justified like when a country is trying to win a war. You can't tell the bad guys where your subs are. But I don't think it was justified in this case.

Later Marlow says 'the only thing one can hope for in life is some sort of self-knowledge.' Maybe he thought the fiancée was a stupid girl, incapable of self-knowledge. After all, in those days men ran the world. Unfortunately."

"Unfortunately is right!" Ms. Harris gave Heidi a thumbs up.

"Reverse sexism!" Jeff Bridges called out. "Prejudice, prejudice."

"History, history," Ms. Harris responded. Then, she threw her head back, and cackled.

After last-period class, Aimy walked Dennie to the pay phone. Dennie called her mom and explained that she was staying after school to meet with Ms. Harris.

"Call me late tonight," Aimy said after Dennie finished her call. "I'll be home about 10:30. After we close, Sean and I are going to get ice cream cones."

"You like Sean, huh?" Dennie's comment was more of a statement than a question.

"Yep," Aimy laughed. "Now that I'm free of Brak. But Sean thinks I'm his little sister. I need to change that."

"Good luck," Dennie said.

"You're the one who needs luck this afternoon. Harris scares me!"

"Pray for me," Dennie sighed.

"She'll eat you alive, Density. She'll suck your blood," Aimy shook her head.

"I wish I had a Webster."

"Density, what are you talking about?"

"You don't remember, do you? When we first met. Mrs. Spinelly. The spider. The Webster."

Aimy cracked up. "Density, you have a memory like an elephant! I was such a dumb kid. I haven't thought about that for years."

"You weren't dumb, Aim. You were adorable."

"Den, you better go or Harris *will* suck your blood. I'll pray for you."

Dennie pointed at herself, put two fingers in the air, then pointed at Aimy. "Me too, you," the signal meant. It had been their signal since elementary school. *See you later.* Me too, you. *I'll miss you.* Me too, you. *I need you.* Me too, you. *I love you.* Me too, you.

CHAPTER 12

Fruits and Thorns

The door to Ms. Harris's classroom hung open. Dennie slipped in. The silence of the room surrounded Dennie. Where was Ms. Harris? Dennie found a seat and pulled her paperback copy of *Heart of Darkness* out of her backpack and began reading. She didn't look up when the click of Ms. Harris's high heels crossed the tile. She didn't notice her teacher watching her as the strings of plot, character, and theme wove together in Dennie's mind, capturing her attention like a butterfly within a net.

But even though the novel held Dennie captive, there were things she hated about it. She hated the dark imagery, the portrayal of natives stripped of their dignity and will. She detested the evil Kurtz who became a servant of his own hellish whims. But most of all, she hated Kurtz's intended because of her inhuman innocence, because she was "deaf and blind to anything but heavenly sights and sounds." But Dennie sort of liked Marlow. He was OK. She read until she finished the story.

"So, Dennie." Ms. Harris strode toward Dennie, her voice ringing out the instant Dennie closed the book. "Why do *you* think Marlow lied to Kurtz's intended?"

"You can't tell someone like her the truth," Dennie said quietly. "She closed her eyes to all of the terrible things in the world."

"Do you think she was justified in doing that?"

Dennie spoke slowly, her eyes meeting her teacher's. "Other people have to live through terrible things, even though they don't want to. Her attitude like—it like erases those people."

"Exactly!" Ms. Harris smiled at Dennie with real warmth. "Like

Marlow says, earth 'is a place to live in, where we must put up with sights, with sounds, with smells, too, by Jove!— breathe dead hippo, so to speak, and not be contaminated.' You're right, Dennie. That woman was a victim of her own chosen innocence, an Eve who never partook of the forbidden fruit. The problem is, this world ain't Eden."

Dennie nodded. She knew that only too well. Suddenly, Ms. Harris's eyes filled with tears. She sniffled loudly. Dennie wasn't prepared for this, not from Ms. Harris, a woman of fire and temper who extracted brilliance from her students like a bee extracts nectar from a dandelion.

"I know these last months have been terrible for you," Ms. Harris gasped. Then, she reached for a kleenex and blew her nose. "But it isn't just today, Dennie. Your recent essays have been mediocre. Cs and Ds when you are capable of As."

"I'll do better," Dennie promised uncomfortably. Did Ms. Harris really care this much?

"Good," Ms. Harris sniffled. "You're a gifted young woman. I want you in my AP class next year. But you've got to bring your grade up."

"OK."

Ms. Harris composed herself, then walked to her desk and retrieved a piece of paper. "I have something for you. Did you know your mother and I both took a university extension course on modern poetry a few years ago? We had to write our own compositions at the end. I kept a copy of your mother's poem because it moved me. Her poem also contains imagery from the Garden of Eden."

Ms. Harris handed the paper to Dennie. With Ms. Harris's eyes on her, Dennie read the poem her mother had written. The poem was titled "Thoughts on Eve While Picking Blackberries."

Blackberries droop
Like pregnant tears
On thorny vines.
To protect myself from thorns
I pull on gloves and pick clumsily,
Crushing some, bruising all.

I tear the gloves away.
Thorns sting my fingers,
Staining them red; berry juice
Mixes with blood.
Yet, fruit fills my basket,
Undamaged. Whole.

I smile wryly, remembering Eve.
Fruit that brought blood seemed
The enemy in Eden.
Yet, in this world of
Lost paradise
It is not so.

And so I labor on.
The miracle of fingertips,
Nerve endings allowing me
To feel
To touch—
The fruit and the thorns.

Dennie stared at the poem. She wasn't sure she understood it. She didn't know exactly why Ms. Harris was crying or what she was thinking. But she did know that Ms. Harris cared. She hadn't kept Dennie after school simply because she was disappointed in her. She had also kept Dennie after to talk to her. Ms. Harris's voice interrupted her thoughts. "Dennie, give your mother my regards. Tell her I remember that poem and I am thinking of her."

"Ok." Dennie left the classroom feeling less detached than usual. Inwardly, she committed to do better. She would focus more and contribute more.

"Remember I'm here, Dennie, if you need me," Ms. Harris called after her. A ray of warmth spread through Dennie. She heard Ms. Harris blow her nose and sniffle once more.

Dennie was lost in her thoughts as she crossed the nearly empty parking lot and headed towards her car. She thought of Ms. Harris and of her mother, of the blackberries and the Garden of Eden. She was taking her keys from her purse when it happened. Dennie's head smashed against the windshield. Pain tore through her arm. Her keys clattered on the pavement. Someone had been waiting for her. Someone had twisted her arm behind her back and pushed her against the car. She couldn't move. She couldn't breathe. His weight crushed her. Why? Why?

"I've been waiting a long time to talk to you, Den-nee." It was Brak's voice in her ear and Brak's breath on her neck. Could his hatred shatter her eardrum? "I know who was behind that letter," he growled. "I know it wasn't Aimy. You've always looked at me like I was dirt."

Physical fear swallowed Dennie. Inner voices screamed. Heavenly Father! Daddy! Mommy! Thes! Help me! Help me! Someone! Please! Anyone!

Then, Dennie heard the sound of a car approaching. Hurry. Hurry.

"We'll talk more later, Den-nee!" He pushed her once more and was gone. Her cheek burned. Her arm ached. The car came nearer. Keep coming. Don't go. Don't go. She kept her balance and turned around. The car approached and stopped in a nearby parking place. She gazed at the vehicle that had answered her prayers and realized that it was a sedan with tinted windows—the same car that had taken her brother to the ocean—the car that had held the cans of beer—the car that had parked outside her house on the night of the King's game—Ty Edwards's car.

As Ty stepped from his car, Dennie's ragged thoughts focused on how different his looks were from Brak Meyers. Ty was average height and heavily muscled; his eyes and coloring were shades of hazel, brown, and tan. So innocent looking. So deceptive. Brak was tall and slim, black haired and light complexioned with eyes like blue steel. Steel so cold and sharp that it could cut without remorse. Who was more dangerous?

Ty Edwards looked at Dennie Fletcher. Why was she standing there like she was in shock, rubbing her arm? What was that look in her eyes? Anger? Hatred? Fear? He spoke. "Dennie, are you Ok? Are those your keys?" He bent down, picked them up and handed them to her.

"How did you know I was here?" she asked.

"I live down the street. Your mom called and asked me to check on you. To make sure your car was still at the school. I guess you had stayed longer than she thought you would."

Dennie didn't say anything. Ty's eyes searched her face. "I want to talk to you about Thes. About the day he died."

"I already know you lied, Ty. I'm not weak like Kurtz's intended. My parents don't know, but I do. Don't try to wipe away your guilt by confessing to my mom and dad. Stay away from us." Her voice shook.

Ty looked down, too hurt and stunned to respond. He clenched his fists. He felt again the helplessness, the horror of that day. And there was the ache, the ache that never went away. He had lied, not to hurt, but to help. He spoke, "When Thes died it felt like I was in a war. Remember what Heidi said. Sometimes when people are fighting a war, they have to lie. Sometimes your mom calls me, Dennie. I can't stay away when she calls."

"The war's over. My mom doesn't need you. She has me." Then, Dennie turned around, climbed into the car and shut the door.

Dennie stopped by Kmart on her way home. She went into the bathroom. She washed her face until the shaking stopped. She brushed her hair and put makeup over the bruise on her cheek. I can't be weak anymore, Heavenly Father, she whispered, not anymore.

When Dennie got home, her mother met her at the front door. Dennie hugged her fiercely, but she did not cry. Her mother hugged her back, feeling the flush of her daughter's cheek, stroking her daughter's hair, wondering what precipitated the hug, and wanting to stretch the moment, to keep the feel and smell of this daughter close to her forever.

"How did things go with Ms. Harris?" Meryl Fletcher studied Dennie after the hug ended. "Dennie, is that a bruise on your cheek?"

"Someone opened a door into me." Dennie shrugged. To avoid her mother's glance, Dennie fished the poem out of her pocket. "Mom, Ms. Harris gave me a copy of a poem you wrote a long time ago. She said the poem touched her and she wanted you to know that she is thinking about you." Dennie handed her mother the poem. As Meryl Fletcher scanned it she felt the tears again, the tears that wouldn't leave her alone.

Dennie hugged her again. "Don't cry, Mommy. I'm here."

"I know," Meryl said. "You are like the fruit, Dennie. So sweet and whole. And strong. I pray for strength like yours. It's just that I never imagined that the thorns could be so sharp."

CHAPTER 13

Leftover People

Right after Aimy moved in across the street, she started hanging out with Thes and me after school. We did our homework together, ate a snack together, and watched reruns of Star Trek until Moni got home from work or Mom shooed us outside. Aimy's new stepfather, Bill, was out of town during the week driving a big rig. Moni worked full time as a beautician.

Moni would come home from work around five. She would stop by our house to get Aimy. I remember her standing in the threshold with a smile that was shy, hopeful, and expectant all at once. Often, she would bring cool snacks for my family, things like pot stickers from Chou's or fresh-fruit slushes from Uncle Marlio's. Sometimes in the evenings I'd go home with Aimy and Moni. Moni would play rock music and feed us hot dogs. She was more like a friend than a mom. She loved to experiment with our hair, braiding it in cool ways, dying a streak of it red or green. She'd give us manicures and pedicures.

But things were different when Bill came home for the weekends. Aimy and Moni stayed home. Sometimes, when Thes and I were outside, we could hear Bill shouting. On one such occasion, Thes turned towards me. "Stay away from that man, Dennie," he warned. "He's a bad man. Don't go there when he's home."

"I won't," I promised. "Poor Aimy. She can't stay away."

"Someday she'll get away," Thes's brows met. "Someday we'll help Aimy get away."

One Saturday, Dad walled off our third-car garage so that we could use it for storage. It had a small window and was like a little room. I told Dad that I thought it would be the perfect place for a puppy to sleep at night. Dad laughed and explained that he couldn't handle a puppy peeing on his lawn or digging in his roses, maybe an adult dog, someday, one that was already trained. I knew that "maybe" was a nice way of saying "don't count on it."

About a month later, on a Sunday afternoon, Mom and Dad went to choir practice. Thes and I were home alone. I thought I heard a puppy whimpering in the backyard. I went outside. The sound was coming from the playhouse. I opened the door. I screamed when I saw Aimy huddled in the corner, in her nightshirt and underwear, with a pair of scissors in her hands. She had chopped off half of her long hair. There was a bruise on her cheek. "Bill hurt me," she sobbed. "Moni didn't help me."

I hugged Aimy. Half of her hair was short and half of it was long. Gently, I took the scissors from her and cut off the rest of her hair. "Thes will know what to do," I promised.

I got a blanket for Aimy and wrapped it around her. We went inside and talked to Thes. He said Aimy could live in our third-car garage until he figured out what to do. I held Aimy's hand while Thes found a camping mattress and a sleeping bag. We made a bed for her in the extra garage, nestled between the boxes. I brought her food and a flashlight. I lent her clothes. I gave her a stack of books. Thes told her not to worry, Mom and Dad hardly ever ventured into the extra garage. He'd figure out an alarm system. When our parents got home, Thes and I were playing checkers as if nothing had happened.

Later that evening, a frantic Moni came over and asked if we had seen Aimy. Thes and I lied to the adults. We told them that we hadn't seen Aimy all day. I even cried. Dad assured me that Aimy would be found.

After dark, we heard police sirens scream to Aimy's house. The next morning, news of the kidnapping flashed on the television and shuddered through the community. We stayed home from school. While Mom and Dad went across the street to join Moni and Bill in their desperate vigil, Thes, Aimy, and I played the board game 'Life.' We fed Aimy some of the casserole Mom had made for her bereaved mother and stepfather. That afternoon, the police came over and asked us all sorts of questions about where Aimy liked to hang out and who she talked about. Where had we last seen her? We answered them with large, innocent, lying eyes. I cried again. Everyone thought it was because of worry, not guilt.

The next morning, the search deepened. Bill and Moni were taken to the police station for polygraph tests. By late afternoon Bill was the prime suspect. By dinnertime, he had disappeared. That evening Moni fell apart at the seams, swallowing tranquilizers, sobbing to reporters, wearing sunglasses to cover her swollen eyes, picking at her fingernails until they were shredded. I was terrified, sure that the police would eventually send Thes and me to prison for kidnapping, if Bill didn't come back and murder us first.

When Mom and Dad were across the street with Moni, Thes and I went out in the garage to talk to Aimy. Bill was gone now, we explained. Did she want to go home? Aimy looked so confused, small, and pale as she lay on her bed between the boxes. It was as if the darkened garage diminished her. Aimy sat up and reached for Mom's sewing kit. (The kit was in storage because Mom hates to sew.)

"You can tell your fortune by using a pencil, thread, and two needles," Aimy said softly as she picked up a pencil next to the mattress and opened the sewing kit. "You stick a threaded needle into the eraser." She demonstrated. "Then, you attach the other needle to the opposite end of the thread. You hold the pencil and let the needle at the bottom dangle. You ask it a question. The needle will start moving by itself. When it moves in a circle, the answer is 'yes.' When it moves back and forth, the answer is 'no.'"

Thes and I gathered around Aimy. She held the contraption in the center of the three of us. I remember how steady her hand was. Why wasn't she shaking? I was shaking. "Should I go home to Moni?" she asked. In a silence thicker than darkness we stared at the dangling needle. It started to move just as the garage door opened.

Dad gaped at us. I had never seen such a shocked expression on anyone's face. It was as if he saw ghosts. He had come into the garage in search of sheets for the extra double bed. (Mom had insisted Moni stay the night.) Instead of finding sheets, he found Aimy and his criminal children.

"Aimy!" Dad gasped. When he had gained his bearings, he picked Aimy up and carried her inside. Thes and I followed dumbly. Mom and Moni were in the living room. At the sight of her daughter Moni ran over, sobbing and smothering Aimy with tears and kisses. Aimy pulled away. "Your hair! Your hair!" Moni sobbed. Mom called the police. Dad stared at Thes and me like he didn't know us. Detectives arrived. Reporters materialized. An ambulance took Aimy and Moni to the hospital.

Detective Schraeder asked Thes and me lots of questions. Thes had to answer because I kept crying. I was afraid of what the police would do to us. I was scared of the look on Daddy's face, the deep crease in his forehead, the tight wrinkle lines around his mouth.

"Where did you find Aimy?" Detective Schraeder questioned.

"In the playhouse," Thes answered.

"How long had she been with you?"

"Since Sunday."

"Why did you hide her?"

"She was afraid to go home."

"Why did she run away?"

A shrug.

"Dennie and Thes," the officer said gently, not even a hint of exasperation in his voice. "Please try to tell us why you hid Aimy?"

I sobbed and said I was sorry. Mom wrapped her arms around me protectively. Thes looked at his hands, then up at the officer. "I hid her because I am her friend," he said stoically.

Dad could barely keep his voice under control. "Didn't you notice how frantic Moni was? Didn't you care that all of the adults in the community were sick with worry? Does lying bother you?"

A little while later, the telephone rang. Dad answered it and handed it to the officer. "We have other evidence now," Detective Schraeder looked levelly at my dad. "Bringing Aimy here might have been the best thing your boy could have done." Then, I realized that the officer already knew why Aimy had run away in the first place.

Aimy, Thes, and I were kept home from school for the next week to protect us from the media. When Aimy and I returned to Mrs. Spinelly's class she treated us as if nothing had ever happened. She insisted the class follow suit. But the kids at school thronged around Thes. He was a kidnapper, a hero, someone unafraid to defy those in power (adults) to protect the powerless (kids). My brother loved the attention.

But Moni was never the same again. She had headaches that would last for days. She kept missing work and had to move her business from one beauty salon to the next until she ended up giving massages and braiding hair with beads at The Gemini Store. Now that Aimy's hair was short, she never offered to do mine again.

Ron picked Dennie up at nine o'clock on Saturday morning. "We're going to stop by my house and get Elise before we see the horses," Ron explained as they turned into the Babcock neighborhood. As they pulled up to Ron's house, Dennie noticed that the remembered roll of toilet paper, dirty and rain-soaked, was still lodged in the evergreen. She giggled.

"What's so funny?" Ron asked, grinning at her.

"Nothing. Really."

"Nothing, huh?" Ron gave Dennie a sideways look. Her laugh had given him courage. He grabbed her hand as they walked toward the front door. Her fingers felt small, cold, and dry in the chill morning air. A toddler's wail rang from the house. "When Elise flew in last night, she surprised us by bringing Jolyn, Sarah's baby," Ron explained. "Jolyn flew for free and it gave Jeff and Sarah a weekend alone. My mom was so excited to see the baby that she started crying and stuff."

Ron and Dennie followed the wails into the kitchen where a solitary thirteen-month-old baby screamed in a yellow high chair. The remains of breakfast littered the countertop—a half-eaten piece of toast, a soggy bowl of cereal, dollops of honey. Ron walked up to the baby, her face and scalp bright red from screaming, her head topped with a sprinkling of fine white hair. Tears swam in Jolyn's light blue eyes as she stretched chubby arms towards Ron. "Hey, Jo, Jo, what's wrong? How come they left you all alone?" Ron asked as he picked her up.

She hiccuped and took a shivering breath. "Du! Du!" She whined.

"Du, du? Ah, you want juice, juice," Ron interpreted.

"You speak *baby*?" Dennie teased.

"A hidden talent," Ron looked at Dennie and grinned, a wide, joyful grin. This was the Dennie he had dreamed about, relaxed and smiling, framed by the morning sunlight streaming through the window. Ron swooped Jolyn around the kitchen making up his own words to the song *The Power of Love*. "You are my baby and I am your fan," he sang, "Whenever you reach for juice, I'll do all that I can." Jolyn squealed and laughed. Ron flung open the refrigerator door, grabbed a juice bottle, threw it into the air, caught it, and presented it to the baby. Jolyn curled her lips around the nipple and sucked loudly.

Tammy pranced into the kitchen. After a quick "Hi, Dennie," she possessively grabbed the baby from Ron. "Come with Aunt Tammy, Jolyn, it's time to get dressed."

The bottle of juice tumbled from Jolyn's fingers. "Du! Du!" the baby wailed.

"Don't worry," Tammy clucked. "Aunt Tammy will pick up your du-du for you." She expertly balanced the baby on her hip while reaching down and scooping up the bottle of apple juice.

"Why don't you pick up the dog's du-du while you're at it, Tam?" Ron suggested.

"Shut up," Tammy said as she sweetly stroked the baby.

"Where's everybody?" Ron asked.

"Mom went to get whole milk at the store because babies need whole milk until they are two. The fat in the milk is important for human brain development. It might help you too, Ronny, since your brain is underdeveloped."

"Funny, Tam," Ron snorted. "Where's Dad and Elise?"

"Mike came and picked up Elise. They took Gretchen. Dad is still asleep. I'm in charge of Jolyn."

"See ya, Jo, Jo." Ron bent down and kissed his niece, adding, "Tammy, here, is great with du-du." Then, he grabbed Dennie's hand and flew with her to the front door.

They drove east of the Babcock's home and out into the countryside. The grassy rolling hills were green from winter rain. "The grass is shimmering today," Dennie commented as Ron drove.

"What?" Ron asked.

Dennie explained. "Uncle Blake showed me shimmering grass a long time ago. He said it happens when the dew, the wind, and the morning sun mix just right. I'll steer, Ron," Dennie said as she reached for the wheel. "Look closely at the fields. You can see lights flickering in the grass, like stars." Ron looked. He couldn't believe that he had never noticed how grass could shimmer! Wow! He took Dennie's hand off the wheel and held it tightly.

Ron turned down Grenacre Lane and drove about a half mile until they came to a large colonial-style home, with white fences, high gables, and a pillared porch. It reminded Dennie of a southern mansion. She could picture Rhett Butler and Scarlett O'Hara emerging. Dennie knew that Sister Allen lived there with her husband, Glenn, whom Dennie had never met since he wasn't active in the Church. But Dennie remembered Mike Carlo, Sister Allen's son from a previous marriage. Mike was tall and slender with dark, long-lashed eyes, as romantic a figure as anyone in *Gone With the Wind.* His girlfriend was Elise, Ron's thin, sweet, older sister, who had a mass of strawberry-blond hair and bright-green eyes.

Ron led Dennie around the house and behind the barn. They found Mike and Elise standing near a fenced arena, where Glenn Allen was working with a mustang. Elise and Mike turned when they heard the other couple approach. "Hi, Dennie," Elise's eyes smiled when she spoke. The look in Elise's eyes was so sweet and open that it reminded Dennie of the look in her mother's eyes, the look she had so often before Thes died. If her parents had been able to have children, would they have had a daughter like Elise? Would they have had a goofy, charming son like Ron?

Mike's voice broke into Dennie's thoughts. "Glenn was able to rescue six mustangs from a herd of about twenty-four. The rest of the herd was slaughtered execution style by high-powered rifles in January. Two mares and four colts survived. Glenn plans to tame them and find homes for them."

Dennie watched the two figures in the arena. The man, Glenn Allen, middle-aged and graying, had a tightly molded physique like her father's, except larger. He stood in the center of the pen, wearing cowboy boots, jeans, and a dusky-gray sweatshirt, the same color as his eyes. A soft cotton rope lay coiled in his hands. He spoke gently to the mare, clicking his tongue. The brown mare, filthy and mud-caked, with wild, panic-riddled eyes, galloped around the perimeter, driven by terror, preferring the cold boundary of the fence to the human menace in the center. Glenn Allen steadily advanced.

"Poor scared baby," Elise whispered.

The mare halted, nostrils flaring, foreleg muscles quivering. She turned toward the man, her body language screaming the need to bolt. Glenn stopped. The mare stood still. Slowly, he uncoiled the rope, then tossed it over her back. The mare spun away leaving the rope in the dirt.

Glenn coiled the rope and strode over to the group of young people. "Elise, do you want to try?" he asked. Elise nodded.

"Whenever the horse turns to you, stop advancing," Glenn instructed. "That way she figures that coming toward you is better than running. A rope hasn't touched her before today, so toss it on her back whenever you get a chance. Try for small gains and end on a positive note."

"OK," Elise said. She took the rope from Glenn and slid into the pen. Gretchen, who had been lying at Elise's feet, whined. Dennie bent down to stroke the dog. Gretchen settled quickly, licking Dennie's fingers. Dennie stood back up and watched as Elise worked with the mare.

"Ron, I've never met your friend," Glenn Allen said suddenly.

"This is Dennie Fletcher," Ron rested his arm on Dennie's shoulder.

"It's nice to meet you, Dennie," Glenn said, shaking Dennie's hand. "I went to a few of Grantlin High's football games this fall. Three years ago, Mike here quarterbacked for the Eagles, so whenever he's in town we catch a game. I was really impressed by the way your brother played. His rushing was tremendous. I don't know if I've ever seen a kid his size run like that. I was shocked when I heard about his death. I'm so sorry."

"I'm sorry too," Mike said. "I keep thinking about your family."

Dennie nodded a thank you. She bit the inside of her lower lip. These people were so kind. They cared about her even if they didn't know her. They were the antithesis of Brak. They saved wild horses. They told the truth. She didn't feel good enough to be with them. She watched the golden, wheat-colored Elise with her soft, steady voice coaxing the mare. She heard Gretchen yawn at her feet. Ron sang softly in her ear, "You are my Dennie, and I am your friend. Whenever you need to talk, just reach for my hand." Dennie smiled and squeezed Ron's fingers. The grass shimmered and the cool breeze strengthened her.

That night, Dennie called Aimy. She told Aimy about her day. She described the shimmering grass, the mustangs, and the lunch Sister Allen made for everyone. She even admitted that she was beginning to have feelings for old Ronny-boy.

"I'm happy for you, Density," Aimy said. Then Dennie described her encounter with Brak. She warned Aimy to be careful and to keep her doors locked when she was home alone. Aimy didn't respond. She was absolutely silent.

"What's up with Sean?" Dennie asked in an effort to break the silence.

"Nothing, absolutely nothing," Aimy answered. "He says I'm his little sister in the gospel. Barf."

"Maybe if you give it time," Dennie suggested.

Aimy didn't answer. Then, abruptly, in a small voice, Aimy changed conversational gears. "Den, do you think there were leftover people in the pre-existence?"

"I don't understand," Dennie said.

"I mean when Heavenly Father planned all of the families in the pre-existence, were people left over? Did he stick them here and there, wherever there was room, in ghettos, in dungeons, with messed-up families like mine?"

Dennie pictured the natives in *Heart of Darkness*, the refugees on the news, the children in the Chilean jail, herself and Thes. Were they all leftover people? She thought about the herd of mustangs slaughtered execution style. Were there leftover animal spirits too? But they weren't leftover animals to Glenn Allen and Elise Babcock. They were important and real. "I don't know, Aim. At church they teach us that everyone is unique with a purpose. I mean, look where Thes and I came from. Were we leftovers too?"

"No, you guys are sealed to your parents. You just came a different route."

"Aimy, maybe Heavenly Father put you in your family to help Moni because you are stronger and better than most people."

"No, Dennie. I'm a leftover person."

"You're not a leftover person, Aimy! You're my friend!"

CHAPTER 14

Our Own Cartilage

One Sunday morning, a few months after Bill left, Aimy, smelling like lemon juice and wearing a skirt and T-shirt, met us in the driveway as we were leaving for church. "Can I go with you?" she asked.

Mom and Dad glowed with delight. "Of course, sweetheart! Of course!" Aimy swept into the backseat of the car between Thes and me. She crossed her legs. Thes kicked her shoe off. Aimy slid it back on and crossed her legs again. Thes kicked it off again. Over and over, on the way to church, on the way home from church, crossed legs, shoe on, shoe off, lemon juice for perfume, week after week, year after year.

Then, when Aimy was thirteen, she decided to be baptized. The service was held on a Saturday morning, during early spring. I still remember how the morning air smelled cool and moist, like seeds in the earth waiting to sprout. The sky was layered, reminding me of Grandma Elsa's trifles. Fog skimmed the ground like smoke. Above it, the air was clear and cool. Next there was a fine, higher mist, and highest of all, the globe of sun radiated, as if it were determined to erase the moisture and claim the day.

Aimy rode with us to the church. The building was unusually cold when we arrived. The missionaries were already there, rubbing their arms. They had turned on the heater, but it would take awhile to warm things up. Aimy dipped her toe in the baptismal font and grinned. "Warm!" she yelled like she was celebrating. I went into the bathroom with her while she changed into a white jumpsuit. Her cheeks flushed as she danced around the bathroom in her baptismal clothes. It was like her slender body couldn't hold all of the energy and hope inside.

Moni arrived while we were singing the opening song. She dabbed at her mascara-ringed eyes until the smeared makeup made them look *bruised. Karin Parker was there too. She was new in the ward and had recently been called as our Beehive adviser. Chris was four years old then. He wore knickers and a white shirt. He wiggled spastically throughout the service. (He hasn't changed much.)*

Elder Lawsen spoke. Then, Elder Calvine baptized Aimy. She picked him because he was so handsome.   After the baptism, I helped Aim change into a silky blue-green dress, fitted around the hips, but flared at the bottom. "My sea-foam dress," she laughed. "Moni bought it for me." It swished around her ankles when she walked out of the dressing area. Thes gave a very short talk on the Holy Ghost. I sang a solo. Then Dad confirmed Aimy a member of the church and she received the gift of the Holy Ghost. After the closing prayer, the elders pushed open the accordion-like dividers revealing the adjacent room with tables full of punch and cookies.

I remember biting into a Rice Krispy treat as I eavesdropped on Uncle Blake's conversation with Karin Parker. "I just finished a teaching credentialing program," Karin smiled. "I was hired in January to teach kindergarten at Alta Elementary. Tell me about you!"

"I'm a nurse," Uncle Blake said. "A male nurse. How 'bout that?"

"That's great! Now, where'd my little boy take off to?" Karin's gaze scanned the room.

"Running the halls," Uncle Blake chuckled.

"I can't keep track of that kid. I felt like my shushing him disturbed the whole baptism."

"No, no," Uncle Blake reassured. Then, he called to Thes and me. "Thes, Dennie, would you guys find Chris for Karin?"

The sliding door separating the baptismal font from the rest of the room had been closed and locked. But we still had access to that area if we went through the side door that led to the dressing rooms and bathrooms. Thes suggested we look there first. After that, we could search the halls.

But we didn't have to search the halls. Chris was in the font! Someone had forgotten to drain the water. Chris had stripped down to his underwear. He had a problem though because he wasn't tall enough to touch the bottom. He solved it by leaping, frog-like, taking a quick breath, and going back under again. We found him doing that, leaping around the water, surfacing with each jump and grabbing a breath of air. We cracked up and Thes dubbed him "frog boy."   But a few seconds later, the little guy missed his mark and didn't jump high enough. Did he breathe in water instead of air? Thes flew into the font and pulled Chris to safety. The little boy choked. His lips were bluish from the cold. Thes pounded his back and he coughed and started crying.

Dripping, Thes carried Chris to Karin. She turned absolutely white. Blake pulled a chair over and she dropped into it and took Chris into her arms. She didn't spank him or yell at him. She just folded him up in her arms. Chris hid his face in his mother's blouse. Mom brought a towel and wrapped it around him. Dad ran to drain the font. The bishop looked nearly as pale as Karin did.

Then, Aimy threw her head back and laughed. She ran up to Thes and hugged him. She kissed his cheek. "Thessie, the Holy Ghost must have whispered Chris was there! You hero!" She exclaimed. Aimy's sea-foam dress swished around Thes's wet ankles. Mom hugged Thes too. Teary-eyed, Karin thanked him. On the way out to the car, Dad thumped Thes on the back. "I'm proud of you, son!" he said.

On the morning of President's Day, Karin invited Dennie to go with her to the Haltsburg auction to "check out wedding stuff." On the way there, Karin told Dennie how she wanted a bright wedding, with big yellow sunflowers decorating the food table, pale yellow tablecloths, and white daisies and yellow roses in her bouquet.

"But, putting it all together swamps me," she added. "I want something unique for table centerpieces, something that people will remember, something different and wonderful. Maybe we'll see something at the auction that will scream out 'Buy me! I'm perfect for Blake and Karin's wedding!'"

"I hope so," Dennie smiled.

"Dennie," Karin chatted, "Being engaged to Blake is like a dream come true for me. I never thought this much happiness would come my way. But sometimes it scares me too. All of the changes. Living so close that you find out each other's secret fears and weird little habits. Then there's Chris. When he gets tired and frustrated, he has a meltdown. I mean he totally melts down. He lays down on the floor and screams and kicks like a two-year-old. I wonder if that will drive Blake crazy?"

"When Thes and I were little, Uncle Blake was pretty patient with our meltdowns," Dennie assured. As they drove on, Dennie kept thinking about how Karin had mentioned secret fears. Dennie's own fears haunted her. She was afraid of her parents finding out the truth about Thes. She was afraid to pray—afraid of the questions she ought to ask and afraid of the answers that could come. And now, after the incident with Brak, she was frightened of being alone. She now scanned the streets, looked over her shoulders, stared out rearview mirrors. She knew Brak was somewhere, following her, ready to materialize. The fear made her palms sweat and her heart beat fast. It had the power to immobilize her. How she longed to tell someone, to feel strong, protective arms around her. But not her parents' arms. They had enough worry, enough fear. And Uncle Blake? His arms belonged to Karin now. But what about Ron Babcock? Could she tuck herself safely in his arms? Would he understand?

"Karin, how did you know Blake was the right one?" Dennie suddenly asked.

Karin was thoughtful before she spoke. "Dennie, my first marriage was so wrong that for a long time I was afraid to *believe* that there was a right one. I married right out of high school—a handsome marine I met at a dance. My parents were wary. They didn't like the way he criticized every little thing, my clothes, the things I said, my hair when I got up in the mornings. We had two babies right away, a little girl, Nicole, then Chris fourteen months later. It was hard keeping up on the clothes and the laundry. I became depressed. Cory, my husband, couldn't control his anger and disappointment.

"Then, we went to counseling and things improved a little bit. That summer, we went camping—Nicole was three and Chris was two. I was making lunch, cooking fish Cory had caught. It was hot. Flies tried to swarm the fish. I was batting them away when I lost track of Nicole. Then, I heard a truck barreling down the lane. I looked up and saw a flash of Nicole's bright-orange swimsuit near the road. I couldn't tell exactly where she was, on which side of the road. I just knew a truck was coming. I screamed her name. She darted across the road, towards my voice, in front of the truck. Cory blamed me for our little girl's death. He never forgave me for calling to her, for causing her to run in front of the truck. He became cruel, Dennie, really cruel. But, I couldn't forgive myself either. One day, while Cory was at work, my parents came over. I put Chris and me and a few of our things into the car. We drove away and never came back.

"For awhile I stayed with my parents. I felt like I was nothing. I felt like I couldn't get up in the mornings. My parents loved me and prayed for me. They put my name on the temple prayer rolls. I went to counseling. Nothing seemed to help. I felt like the world was dark, like I couldn't go on.

"Then, one day as I watched Chris play, I started crying because I wanted my little boy to have joy in his life. He was my son. I wanted him to always have hope. I wanted desperately for him to feel good-ness and courage and forgiveness and joy and light. And then it was like I had a revelation. I realized that I was his mother. He had to see those things in *me*. I went back to school. I made myself smile, laugh, and play with my son. I kept going.

"Then, when I had finally made a life for myself, when I was finally standing on my own feet and supporting my son, I met Blake. First, I was so afraid. I didn't want to do something *wrong* again."

Dennie didn't know what to say. She looked at Karin's hair that was almost orange and her freckled hands. She thought of Karin's guileless smile, her simple white tennis shoes, her tendency to chatter, and the pile of kindergarten papers in the backseat. Karin's car smelled vaguely like spoiled milk. Yet, Karin was strong. She was a rock. And like the rock Moses struck releasing a river of water, it was as if Karin's words struck Dennie's heart, loosing a flood of feelings—shared loss, shared sorrow, shared grief. Dennie cried. Not just tears, but sobs, as jagged and broken as rocky ridges cut out by the ocean.

Karin pulled the car over. She folded her arms around Dennie. "I love you, Dennie," she said. When Dennie's sobs lessened, Karin continued, "Dennie, always remember that things change; life really does go on. Although the memories are always there, like a residue of pain beneath the joy, we can emerge from our personal prisons of fear and death and pain. I think of how the Prophet Joseph Smith suffered terribly in Liberty jail, but with God's help, he survived it and grew spiritually."

"Remember how Chris mixed up Carthage and cartilage?" Dennie said, trying to stop crying, trying to smile. "He is so cute."

Karin stroked Dennie's hair. "Yes, and like a wonderful man once said, 'We all have our own cartilage.' Our cartilage might seem flimsy. But God gave us bones, too, and tendons and ligaments and hope and faith and testimony and each other to hold us together." Then, seventeen-year-old Dennie Fletcher and thirty-something Karin Parker found themselves laughing in each other's arms, laughing through tears.

CHAPTER 15

Little Fish Have Feelings

Mom used to say that in some ways Dad and Thes's personalities were too much alike, while in other ways they were just plain opposites. This disparity caused the chemistry of their souls to clash. "But," Mom explained, "that doesn't mean they don't love each other. That doesn't mean they aren't wholly committed as father and son." Still, their relationship was like an allergy that affected the whole family—like an underlying tiredness, a nagging cough, a feeling of not being entirely well. Yet when Dad and Thes went fishing at the ocean, it was like the salty sea breeze swept away the pollen in the air. They were father and son. They were one.

As a family, we would camp at Salt Point, a state park north of Jenner where the cliffs were jagged and rock formations jutted far out into the ocean. Mom and I often hiked out onto the rocks and watched Dad and Thes fish. When I was in junior high I would fish with them. But one night, following an afternoon when I had hooked two bottom fish, I dreamed that the fish grew arms, and legs. These sad-eyed quasi-human creatures tried to talk to me, but had no voices. After that, I lost my desire to fish.

But Thes and Dad loved it. They would hike way out on the rocks during the low tides, bamboo fishing poles in hand, creels swinging from their shoulders, buckets containing squid bait dangling from their calloused fingers. Mom loved to sit on a rock with her pen and paper in hand, watching Thes and Dad in the distance, ready to compose the one poem that she never wrote.

I think she was too busy watching them. She smiled at the way they squatted down next to each other and attached lines and hooks to their *bamboo poles. After that, they worked in tandem, their male blue-jeaned bodies standing strong at the edge of jutting rocks. As a wave receded, they'd lean their poles deep into the water, with the gulls circling overhead eyeing the buckets of bait, and families of sea lions lazing in the water, watchful but relaxed. The ocean roared around them. Then the next wave would come, leaving fish behind. Dad and Thes would pull their crude, makeshift poles from the pools, sometimes hooking sleek ling cod, or bottom fish with bright colors and bulging eyes. When one of them hooked a fish, the other would help land it by giving advice, challenges, chuckles, and, finally, congratulations.*

Sometimes, when the fish were biting, they would stay out too long. The tide would rise. They would have to jump across rock formations, which grew increasingly wet and treacherous with each moment. At these times they stayed close together, warning each other about patches of slippery black seaweed. Once, I watched from the safety of the bluff as they hunkered against a tower of rock while a wave rose like a pregnant whale. They wedged their gear between them and clasped arms around each other's shoulders. The wave broke on the rock and their images disappeared in the foam. When the wave receded, they emerged soaked and laughing, like the sea gods Poseidon and Titan, bearing bamboo scepters and treasure buckets overflowing with fish.

Later, the evening after that fishing trip, Dad asked Thes to help him take down the tent and load the car. Thes ignored Dad. Mom and I helped instead. While we were cleaning up camp, Thes built a fire and put his pants and shoes near it in order to dry them out. When he went to retrieve them, the fire had singed holes in the bottom of his jeans. His shoe soles had melted. Mom and I giggled, but Dad snapped at him. "Why were you building a fire instead of helping to load the car? This wouldn't have happened if you had listened to me! What were you thinking? You'll have to pay for new shoes and pants." Thes climbed in the car and slammed the door. Mom coughed and I blew my nose. Our trip to the ocean was over.

Karin and Dennie had a great time at the auction. They bought huge baskets of silk sunflowers, and pale yellow fabric for table clothes. They found strings of white lights to adorn the silk trees they would borrow. They purchased circular mirrors to set in the middle of the round dining tables, illuminating the centerpieces—the "unique and perfect" centerpieces that were still a mystery, even to Karin.

They took a break, sipping hot chocolate and snacking on onion rings. Karin told Dennie her most embarrassing moment, the time she had gone to a job interview at a school in Sacramento. After using the bathroom, she had emerged with the paper toilet-seat protector caught in the back of her skirt waving like a white flag for the entire school to see. Dennie laughed so hard she choked on her onion ring.

"Something sort of like that happened to me," Dennie said when she could talk. Her sight was blurry from laughing. She wiped her eyes. "Last winter, I grabbed a sweater out of the closet right before church. A hanger was stuck to the back of my sweater but I didn't know it. I sang a solo. I walked all the way to the front of the chapel with that hanger stuck in the back of my sweater. When I turned around to sing, I couldn't figure out why everyone in the congregation was smiling."

"I remember that," Karin grinned. Dennie busted up. "Now," Karin added, "tell me one of Blake's embarrassing moments. I do so many silly things that I'm going to need ammunition once we're married."

Dennie thought for a moment. "This one is lame, but it *was* funny to Aimy and me. Aimy and I were partners for the science-fair project in fifth grade. We decided to do a survey to find out which baby foods tasted the best. We blindfolded Uncle Blake and made him taste different brands of baby food. I spoon-fed him while Aimy took notes and photos for the write-up. Uncle Blake did great tasting the fruits and vegetables, but when we got to the combination dinners, stuff like 'Chicken Noodle Delight' and 'Beef and Potato Surprise,' he couldn't take it. Each time he took a bite, he turned green and nearly gagged. Then, when I spoon fed him the 'Cream of Vegetable Beef Delight' he jerked the blindfold off, ran into the bathroom and threw up! Aimy took a picture of him barfing to document our results!"

Karin giggled, "I'm going to have to make a casserole for him and call it 'Cream of Vegetable Beef Delight.' Do you think he'll remember?" Then, she looked at her watch. "Speaking of science projects, I promised Chris I'd stop by the pet store and buy goldfish for him."

At the pet store, a young clerk with glasses and receding hair led Dennie and Karin to the cold-water fish. Karin explained how her son had instructed her to get two Common Goldfish, two Orandas, and two Ryukins. The clerk told Karin that the Orandas and Ryukins originated in Japan and didn't look anything like the Common Goldfish. He pointed out quarter-sized fish sweeping gracefully through water with wide lacy tails and elegant feathery fins. They were deep orange and snowy white in color.

"They're so pretty!" Karin exclaimed.

While the clerk netted the fish and put them into plastic, water-filled bags, Karin and Dennie checked out the fishbowls. They found quite a variety. The fishbowls came in varying sizes and shapes. One could choose glass or plastic. The store even carried decorative glass fishbowls, the size of grapefruits, with fragile, fluted edges. Karin picked one up and ran her fingers around the edges. She licked her lips. "Dennie, imagine bright-green gravel, a spiraling seashell, floaty ferns and a gorgeous Ryukin gliding around!"

"Are you thinking what I think you're thinking?"

"A table centerpiece! Bright and spring-like! Unique and perfect! Chris will love it too!"

"You could see the reflection of the fish in the mirror," Dennie added excitedly.

"Serendipity!" Karin exclaimed.

On Friday evening, Dennie and Aimy were at work, deep in grease, constructing Beef Burgers. Dennie told Aimy that Karin, Blake, and Chris were stopping by for dinner. She went on to describe her shopping trip with Karin and the decorations they had picked out for the wedding reception.

Aimy balked when Dennie told her about the goldfish. She flipped a row of burgers and exclaimed, "I can't believe Karin's going to have her kid's goldfish swimming around for table centerpieces at Blake's wedding reception. That's crazy! Wedding receptions should be elegant! Has the woman no class?"

"Aim, these fish don't look like normal goldfish. They are really pretty. White and orange. Feathery."

"They sound like Karin. White skin. Orange hair. Feathery. Silly. Stupid."

The hamburger patties sizzled. Dennie put the buns on the grill, her face red, her temperature rising. "Aimy, Karin is not silly and stupid! There's a lot more to Karin than you think. She's been through a lot, and she's done a lot with her life. She's really sweet. I like her!" Dennie flipped the buns over.

Amy went on. "What has she done with her life? Teaching kindergarten is not some great accomplishment! It's mostly wiping kids' noses. Karin has no class. She just lucked out with Blake. When my mom got married she had these elegant centerpieces, deep purple roses in crystal vases. Moni had class."

"Moni married Bill!" The words came out of Dennie's mouth so quickly, before she had time to call them back.

"Shut up!" Aimy shouted as she slammed the hamburgers onto the buns.

"Is there something I can help you ladies with?" Sean called out after hearing Aimy's outburst.

"No!" Aimy shouted back.

"Dennie?" Sean asked. Dennie shook her head with a sick feeling in the pit of her stomach. The door to Beef Burgers opened.

"Dennie, your uncle and company just walked in," Sean added. "Grab some burgers, fries, and shakes for them. Then, take ten."

"Thanks, Sean," Dennie said. She wrapped up some of the burgers that had just been grilled and pulled together a mound of Pig-tail Fries and three Creamy Chocolate Milkshakes. Then, she pulled Blake, Karin, and Chris out of line and went with them to a table.

"Food's on the house!" she said as she passed out the burgers.

"Hey, my hamburger bun is squished," Chris complained.

"For Heaven's sake, Chris! Tell Dennie you're sorry and thank her," Karin corrected.

"Thank you, Dennie. I don't like onions." Chris pulled off the onions with grubby fingers.

Karin went on. "Shh, Chris, these *are* the best burgers in town. Dennie, you look hot. Have some of my milkshake. Here's an extra straw."

Dennie took a sip. "How are you doing, kiddo?" Blake asked her. "Great!" Dennie smiled and sneezed.

"You don't sound so great and your face is all red." Blake touched Dennie's forehead, checking her for fever.

"I'm fine, Uncle Blake. It's almost March. My allergies always start in March."

"Guess what Dennie?" Chris exclaimed showing off teeth full of half-chewed, ketchup-dipped Pig-tail Fries. "I finished my science experiment!"

"So what did you find out?" Dennie encouraged.

"Every single fish made it through the maze faster when they saw their own seashells! Dennie, they wanted their own stuff! My *hyposethis* was correct!"

"*Hypothesis*, son, not *hyposethis*," Karin gently corrected.

"Can you believe it?" Blake said, thumping Chris on the back. "Those little fish have feelings!"

"Wow!" Dennie grinned.

"I think I should get first place!" Chris said.

"Me too," Dennie agreed.

"The important thing is that you learned something," Karin added in her motherly tone. Then, Karin and Blake began talking about honeymoon plans. While his mother's attention was diverted, Chris turned to Dennie, plugged his nose, and in a high whisper imitated Karin, "The important thing is that you learned something." Dennie laughed.

From behind the grill, Aimy stared at Dennie and her family. She felt loneliness seep through her. She had already lost Thes, Brak, and any hope of a real relationship with Sean. Now, she was losing Dennie, her best friend, to Karin Parker and Ron Babcock. She had lost her mom a long time ago when Moni had become so absorbed in medicating her own hurt that she couldn't be a mother anymore. Sean came up behind Aimy and put his hand on her shoulder. "Hey, what's bothering ya'll?"

Aimy ignored him. He thought of her as a little girl. He wasn't even worth an insult. She turned back to the grill. *I hate Karin Parker*, she thought. *But why?* Why did Karin irritate her so much? Then, Aimy knew. She hated Karin because Karin had found a way to go on when Moni hadn't. Because Karin and Chris had a family now and Aimy had nothing.

CHAPTER 16

The Weather of Souls

A year and a half ago, Mom went in for a base-line mammogram and there they were—tiny lesions called calcifications indicating a little bit of intra-ductal cancer. After the biopsy, Dr. Toom (a great name for a cancer surgeon) explained that the cancer was caught so early that it was ninety-eight percent curable. Nothing to panic about, more like a pre-cancer than a real cancer. The doctor would do a lumpectomy, lay some radiation on the area and bingo, Mom would be fine. Not to worry, all was well. Thank goodness for modern medicine. Thank goodness for early detection. We were stunned.

Mom's surgery was scheduled for Monday, September 13. I'll never forget that day. Mom said goodbye to Thes and me before we left for seminary. She smiled bravely at us. She reminded us that it was outpatient surgery so she would be home before school was out. Thes hugged her tenderly. He didn't start swearing until we were in the car.

"Stop it, Thes!" I responded. "She's going to be OK. She's going to be fine!"

"She's going to the hospital, Dennie! People die in hospitals! People die from cancer!"

"She's not going to die, Thes! She's not even going to the hospital. She's going to the surgery center. Mom's going to be fine."

"It's happened to us before. It could happen again." Thes spoke darkly. I wondered if Thes referred to our mother in Chile? But, he never talked about her. Ever.

"Am I supposed to honk for Aimy?" Thes asked savagely as he backed out of the driveway.

"No, Aimy has a cold. She's not coming this morning."

Thes drove past the church parking lot towards the freeway. "Thes, where are we going?" I asked, feeling shaky. My brother had an angry, driven look in his eyes.

"Not to seminary or school! That's for sure!"

I argued. "If we aren't at seminary, Uncle Blake will tell Mom and Dad. He's meeting them at the surgery center at nine. Mom will worry if she doesn't know where we are. Plus, we need to be where Mom and Dad can get hold of us if they need us, if something goes wrong."

Thes slammed on his brakes and did a U-turn. A moment later our car squealed into the church parking lot. "You don't remember her, do you?" Thes asked when the car halted.

"Who?" I questioned. Thes was silent.

"Mama in Chile?" I said quietly. A barely perceivable nod came from Thes.

I thought for a moment. "I hardly remember anything about her," I admitted. I studied my hands. Were my hands like hers? Who was this woman whose image I couldn't quite pull up from my memory? "Sometimes it seems like a dream. Like she never existed."

"She slept with you when you were a baby! She sang to you!" Thes's voice was like an accusation.

I looked out the window at the orange streaks of dawn. "I don't remember."

"I do," Thes said. "I remember how she left. I remember how she never came back."

"Most of what I remember is you," I said. "How you painted your face with mud. How you made me run towards the star. How you bossed me around. How you took care of me."

"Yeah, and look how good you turned out!" Thes's mood had softened. He punched me lightly in the arm.

"Mom's going to be OK, Thes," I said. "Heavenly Father will take care of her. I know it." Thes nodded, but I knew he still didn't believe me. He was pretending. I knew his eyes too well, his dark eyes that betrayed his fear and anger.

We got out of the car. For a second I wished that we were still little kids—that we could walk hand-in-hand for comfort, for strength. Lautaro and Mina. Thes and Dennie. Brother and sister. Family.

One morning, Pat Babcock, Ron's mother, was looking through the entertainment section of the Haltsburg Herald when she noticed an article about nighttime snowshoeing in the Sierras. It sounded fun and she had been a bit blue this week. She missed her daughters and grandbaby. She read on. A number of resorts offered guided tours once a month when the moon was full. A guide would take groups out into the wilderness after dark, under mountains pillowed with snow, the world resplendent with moonlight. The article explained that a week from Saturday was a full moon. There were phone numbers for reservations.

"Gary," she interrupted the bishop whose consciousness lay buried deep in the sport's section of the newspaper. "Let's take the kids up. It would be so much fun."

The bishop looked at his wife over the top of his wire-rimmed glasses. "I think Ron's planning a date with Dennie that night. It would be just you, me, and Tammy."

"Why not invite the whole Fletcher family? Ron would be thrilled and I'd like to get to know Meryl better. Not to mention Dennie. We should include Aimy Tomlinson too. I know you've been concerned about her."

"Good idea," the bishop nodded. He stood up, stretched and kissed his wife's forehead. It was raining outside. He pulled on his coat. As he backed out the driveway, he thought he saw a dead bird on the front lawn. But as he looked more closely, he realized that it was the roll of toilet paper, fallen from the evergreen, lying limp and soaking on his grass. Images of Dennie and Aimy crowded in his mind. He whispered a silent prayer for the youth in his ward.

Two days later, Aimy was thrilled about the snow trip. This surprised Dennie who had been concerned that Aimy would feel like a third wheel now that Dennie and Ron were dating. "Density, of course I want to go," Aimy said while they talked over the telephone. "Sister Babcock called yesterday and invited me. I couldn't tell her 'no.' She said she saw one of my drawings at the school art show last year. Did you know she does watercolors? She said she'll work with me this summer."

"Aren't you scheduled to work Saturday night?"

"Kari's taking my shift. You know what I'm going to do, Dennie? I'm going to bring a bunch of sparklers that I bought the last Fourth of July and never used. Don't you think Tammy Babcock would have a great time running around with sparklers?"

"Absolutely," Dennie said. "Unless they cause an avalanche." She could feel Aimy's grin beaming through the phone line all the way to her.

The families planned to drive separately to the foothills on Saturday evening. There they would meet at five o'clock at a restaurant called *The Marauder's Den,* have dinner together, then carpool to Hawk Valley where they would rent snowshoes and begin their moonlit tour.

On Saturday, there was a light snow on the ground when the Fletchers (with Aimy) and the Babcocks met for dinner. The sky was overcast, occluding the first hints of the moon. They got out of their cars and walked toward the restaurant together.

"I hope the food's good," Bishop Babcock commented. "Ron's the only one of us who's been here before."

"Trust me!" Ron chuckled. "I came here last summer with Mike and Elise. *The Marauder's Den* has the best food in California."

"You just like the name!" Tammy chirped to Ron. "*The Maurader's Den.* Dennie."

Aimy rolled her eyes and Ron grinned. "You have a point," he said and he took Dennie's hand as the group shuffled into the entrance of the restaurant. A collage of ornately framed old photographs decorated the entryway wall.

"Ron, look!" Tammy exclaimed as she studied the pictures. "Here's a picture of Joaquin Murieta and Three-Fingered Jack! Here's Black Bart! I can't believe it!"

"Yea, Tam, isn't it cool!" Ron laughed his big, relaxed, open laugh. "I think that's why Elise brought me here."

"What on earth do these stagecoach robbers from gold-rush times have to do with you guys?" Aimy asked.

Tammy grabbed Aimy's hand as she explained. "Our Grandpa Sheldon's ancestors settled in California during the gold rush. Whenever we would spend the night, Grandpa would try to scare us by making up stories about the ghosts of Joaquin Murieta, Black Bart, and Three-fingered Jack."

"I remember your grandpa," Dennie said. "He taught me in primary a long time ago. One time we had a class party at his house in the country. It was cool."

"That's where Ron used to search for gold," Tammy teased. "He never found any though."

"Don't tell family secrets!" Ron warned jokingly as he thumped Tammy on the head.

"How long has it been since your father's passing?" Meryl Fletcher suddenly asked Pat Babcock.

"About two and a half years," Pat smiled softly.

"Do you still miss him?" Meryl asked.

Every member of the Babcock family nodded. "He was such a kind, pleasant man," the bishop said.

Pat Babcock lightly squeezed Meryl's hand as she said, "I think we will always miss him. Yet, time has lessened the pain we felt at his passing and we have found comfort and gladness in our memories."

Two hours later, bundled in winter clothes, full from a hearty meal, and wearing light, narrow snowshoes, the group began their trek on Hawk mountain. "Be sure to stay on the trail," cautioned their host, Fred, as he led them out of the rental area into the night. "These mark the trail," Fred continued, pointing to tiny lanterns made of candles and paper. "They'll lead you to a campfire where another host is waiting. You'll dine on s'mores and be entertained by a local guitarist."

As they walked along the trail, the tiny candles caused Dennie to think of the Hansel and Grettel story, of the white stones that marked the children's way through the forest to their home. She wished she could mention this to Thes. She wished he were here. She wondered if her parents were thinking the same thing. Did they remember how much he loved that story? But her parents were talking and laughing with the Babcocks. Anyone watching would have thought that they weren't even thinking about Thes right now. But Dennie knew differently. The reality of Thes's death was like the weather, always present, like a constant rain outside the window of their souls.

Suddenly, a snowball hit Dennie on the shoulder. Aimy grinned at her, the snow on her mittens proof of her guilt. Dennie fired one back. Soon Tammy and Ron joined the battle. They outdistanced the adults, laughing as they plastered each other with snow. But after awhile, the rigor of the hike and the cold of the night quieted them. Tammy trudged back to her parents, while Ron, Aimy, and Dennie walked on. They passed trees whose branches sighed under cushions of snow, and silent creeks set in deep snow-banked inclines. When they finally saw the fire in the distance, Aimy felt a burst of energy surge through her. She clapped her hands together. "Race you!" she challenged. Dennie clomped along, but Ron beat Aimy easily, his long legs pulling snowshoed feet up and down, bouncing across the field of snow.

At the campfire, Aimy pulled the package of sparklers out of her inside jacket pocket and asked the bare-fingered guitarist's permission to light them. When he nodded affirmatively, Tammy yelped with glee. With lights in their hands, Aimy and Tammy whirled, leapt, and sliced the air like Nordic nymphs doing a ritualistic dance.

The adults listened to the guitar music and ate s'mores while smiling in awe at Aimy and Tammy's energy. Ron pulled Dennie off a little way. There he told her the names of the stars, just as his grandfather had taught him long ago. Dennie leaned against him. She wouldn't remember much of what he told her that night for she was thinking about how warm a person could feel on a frigid night in the mountains while the moon hung in the sky like a white plate.

At ten o'clock, when they were back at the lodge, Ron attempted to convince the adults that he should drive Dennie, Aimy, and Tammy down the mountain, back to Grantlin. "That way you guys can stop for hot chocolate, or visit, or whatever," Ron cajoled. Since it was a clear night, the Babcock and Fletcher parents agreed. "What a night to discover whatever *whatever* is!" the bishop added, raising his eyebrows.

For the young people, it was a relatively quiet drive down the mountain. Dennie sat next to Ron. In the backseat, Tammy fell asleep on Aimy's lap within minutes after their departure. Soft rock played on the radio. Dennie and Aimy sang along. Two hours later, when they arrived in the Fletcher's neighborhood, Aimy carefully lowered Tammy's head onto a bunched-up jacket. She liked the feel of the child's soft curls on her fingertips. Maybe someday she would learn to do hair like her mother. "I'll leave you two married people alone," Aimy teased as she positioned herself to open the van's sliding door. But Ron was already out of the van. He ran around to the side, and opened the door for Aimy, then walked her up to her front door.

"Take care of Density, Ronny-boy," Aimy said as she gave Ron a quick hug. He turned and walked back towards the van. A light was on in the kitchen, and for a second Aimy hesitated, imagining that it was the light of a safe and happy home, and that she was as secure and treasured as a princess in a castle. Before going in, she turned around and blew a kiss towards her friends. Ron waved as he climbed into the van.

A block from Aimy's house, Brak Meyers sat stonily in his car. He watched Aimy hug Ron Babcock and blow him a kiss. Hard, dark anger filled him. He thought about how much he wanted her, how she was made for him. He deserved her. She knew that. He had seen it in her eyes a hundred times. Yet, she had turned on him. She had written him that letter. And now she was dating Ron Babcock. Brak's breath quickened as his rage mounted.

He had thought Thes Fletcher was the only person capable of casting a shadow between him and Aimy, but he had been wrong. He remembered when he was a kid and had played with matches. To teach him a lesson, his dad had strapped the matches to his fingers and lit them. His dad hadn't blown them out until Brak felt the heat begin to singe his flesh. Brak had never played with matches again. He had learned. And there was the winter day he had gone outside to play and had refused to wear a coat. His father had locked the house, and for hours Brak had shivered and pounded on the front door. He had never forgotten how cold it was.

He was cold now too. Cold inside. Cold enough to teach Aimy the lesson she needed to learn.

Ron started the ignition, then took Dennie's hand. She was shaking.

"What's wrong?" Ron asked. Dennie pointed to a car parked far down the street. It was a mustang. Ron shook his head. Why was Dennie afraid of a parked car?

"It's Brak Meyer's car," Dennie whispered. "My parents aren't home yet. I can't go in yet, Ron. I can't go in 'til my parents are home."

"Why?" Ron asked.

"Drive somewhere. Anywhere. Then we can talk."

Ron drove down the street. They stopped at Grantlin Park.

Tammy's breathing was light and even in the backseat. Dennie gripped Ron's hand tightly. Then she told him about Brak Meyers. About Ty Edwards. About her brother's death. About her lie. About her fear.

CHAPTER 17

Manna

A month after Mom's surgery, she began radiation treatments. This regimen required trips to the Sacramento Cancer Center five days a week for six weeks. Mom went each afternoon, arriving home right before dinner. She didn't lose her hair or her smile, but as the number of treatments accumulated, she lost a portion of her zest and energy.

During this time period, Dad was extremely busy. He had client deadlines and church commitments. Because of these, he was gone most evenings. It was football season for Thes. My brother worked out constantly and was rarely home. When he was home, his moods were dark. He was less affectionate to mom than ever before. I couldn't understand why he pulled away from her when she needed him most. Mom made a valiant effort to go to his games regardless of how tired she was after her radiation treatments. To intensify matters, Thes never lifted a finger around the house. Dad imposed rules and threats. Thes ignored them. Mom and Dad argued about how to deal with my brother.

On a Friday, Mom's last day of radiation treatments, Dad decided to attend an annual charity event hosted by his biggest client. The event included a golf tournament as well as an evening of dinner and entertainment. I remember Dad saying good-bye when he left that morning. He looked handsome in his creased beige Dockers and new navy golf shirt. He gave Mom a quick hug but she didn't respond. I could sense the tension between them. The previous day they had argued about the golf tournament. Mom had wanted Dad to stay home and have lunch with her to celebrate the successful treatment of her cancer. She also felt that he ought to go to Thes's game.

Dad had said he didn't have a choice. He had to go to this client's event. He felt badly, but it was not only a social obligation; it was his largest client. If the client relationship soured he'd lose a huge chunk of income. "What about your relationship with Thes?" Mom had asked.

Dad got home about eleven o'clock the night of the charity event. Thes was out celebrating a football victory with his friends. I had just gotten home from the game. I told Dad that Mom was in bed. She had been too exhausted to make it to Thes's game. Dad and I watched the highlights of Thes's game on the news. Then Dad said he was going to turn in. I decided to numb out for a few more minutes in front of the TV.

"Goodnight, Denz," Dad said as he started up the stairs. "Night," I waved with my eyes on the screen. Dad climbed the stairs and went into the master bedroom. He didn't turn the light on. Moving in the dark so that Mom could sleep, he felt his way into a white T-shirt and pajama bottoms. He went into the bathroom. He softly closed the door, then flipped on the light in order to brush his teeth. He looked in the mirror. It looked as if he were turning blue! Was it the light? He flexed his muscles and the bluish hue seemed to increase. He looked up. The blue hue of his neck and chin seemed to be deepening.

"Meryl are you awake?" he called.

"Uh-huh," Mom answered.

"Could you come here? Something's wrong with me."

Mom joined him. "I'm turning blue," Dad said with a worried smile. "What could cause this? A stroke? A heart attack? Internal bleeding?"

The color left Mom's face as she sat on the edge of the tub to gain her equilibrium. "Go lay down. I'll call 911," she said. She stood up. She went into the bedroom to call.

"But I don't feel sick or dizzy," Dad said, still staring at himself in the mirror. "Blake's a nurse. Try him first." Dad suggested. Mom dialed Uncle Blake's phone number, but no one was home.

"Blake's working tonight," she said.

"Give me a minute," Dad said as he turned on the water in the bathroom sink.

Mom felt her heart pound. She was afraid that Dad would pass out any moment, afraid that if she didn't get the paramedics here quickly it would be too late. She had seen so many people the past few months with their cancers discovered too late, cancers that could have been defeated in earlier stages. If this had something to do with Dad's heart or a broken artery, or not enough oxygen in his tissues, she had even less time. She began to press the emergency code—911 . . .

"Stop!" Dad shouted. He burst into a jubilant laugh. "It's washing off!"

Mom hung the telephone up and ran into the bathroom. Dad's arms were covered with soap. "I wore a new shirt today," he said. "The dye must have somehow reacted with my skin. It's some kind of stain!"

"It didn't look like a stain," Mom said, still cautious. Dad showed her where some of the blue had washed off.

Then Mom breathed again. A giggle burbled from her. "Rick, can you imagine if the paramedics had come! We would never have convinced them we were intelligent human beings!" At the thought, they both fell into gales of laughter. I heard them and went upstairs to discover the joke. When I found them, they were hugging each other, laughing so hard they were crying, with Dad's wet arms soaking the back of Mom's nightgown. Between gulps of laughter they told me what had happened.

I smiled. It was like the intensity of their fear and relief had washed their relationship clean. They laughed with their arms around each other. My parents' emotions shouted: "We have each other! We love each other! We are safe again!" I told them good night and left the room. They locked their bedroom door behind me. I knew why.

An hour later Thes came home. I was halfway awake when I heard him stumble into the bathroom and throw up in the toilet. I thought he must have the flu. I went in to see if he was all right. The sickening smells of beer and throw-up met me. The look in my eyes must have been similar to Dad's expression years earlier when he found the kidnapped Aimy in his own garage. I stared at Thes in disbelief. This couldn't be happening! This couldn't be my brother! We don't drink in our family. We had made a promise to each other, a promise!

"You're drunk!" I accused him when I found my voice. "Why, Thes? Why?"

Thes looked at me through unfocused eyes. He started to cry. "Mina, I'm scared! Mom's sick. I'm scared, Mina." He threw up again. He looked so frightened and pitiful that I felt sorry for him. I helped him take his shirt off.

He became frantic. "I have to clean up! So they don't know!" I helped him into the shower. I put his clothes in the washing machine.

He sat on the shower floor in his boxer shorts, with his head between his knees as the water pounded him. He heaved again. "Don't tell Mom

I'm drunk," he begged. "I'll stop. I promise." He sobbed. "Promise me, Mina. Promise me you won't tell Mom or Dad. I'll stop. I'll stop. I promise. I promise." I turned off the water. Thes continued to sob as I put a towel around him and cleaned up the bathroom. I made a vow to my brother because he was the one who had fed me and kept me warm.

The night before Blake and Karin's wedding, Dennie was at the church with her family decorating the cultural hall. Karin directed the crew while Chris, up hours past his bedtime and running on nothing but adrenaline, raced across the stage darting in and out of the heavy velvet curtains.

"Karin," Meryl Fletcher called out. "I can't find the scissors. Dennie and I need them to cut this plastic liner for the food tables." Chris let out a whoop.

"Chris, please calm down!" An exhausted Karin begged. Then the little boy, as if this was his cue, leapt from the stage to the cultural hall floor with a pair of scissors in each hand.

"Christopher!" Karin covered her face with her hands while Blake took the scissors from the boy. Blake's voice was firm and clear when he spoke. "Son, don't ever run with scissors in your hands! Your mom and I want you around for the wedding tomorrow." Chris looked up at the man who was soon to marry his mother. Then, he gazed at his tennis shoes.

"I was just helping," the child whined. "Sister Fletcher and Dennie were looking for the scissors."

Half an hour later, the hall was bright with yellow tablecloths, white lights, and green foliage. Chris made jubilant airplane sounds as he raced around the circular dining tables. Meryl touched Dennie's arm. "Hon, could you take Chris on a walk outside? Karin and I will get the centerpieces together. Then, we'll be done."

"Great idea!" Karin brightened.

"I need to stay here and help with the fish!" Chris argued. "I need to make sure they have their own seashells! They will be lonely tonight if they don't have the right seashells!"

"For criminy sakes, Chris!" There was an unusual edge in Karin's voice. "Outside now! Your fish will be fine!"

Dennie steered a reluctant Chris toward the door. "We can play hide and seek in the bushes," she offered.

"It's too dark and windy to play hide and seek," Chris said when they were outside. He was right. The wind plastered Dennie's hair against her face. Chris continued, pointing. "Turn around, Dennie! Look at the parking lot!"

Dennie moved her hair out of her eyes and turned to look. Around fifty blossoming trees bordered the asphalt. The wind had stripped off bunches of their blossoms, and thousands of frail white petals covered the pavement like a light snow.

"Uncle Blake showed us one of these before seminary yesterday," Dennie commented as she picked a petal from the dark pavement. "He told us the petals are probably about the same color, shape, and size as the manna the Israelites ate in the wilderness."

"Were the Israelites the good guys or the bad guys?" Chris asked.

"Definitely the good guys," Dennie said. "They were on their way to the Promised Land. They needed something to eat so Heavenly Father sent a kind of wafer or bread out of the sky. They gathered it in baskets. They called it manna. The word 'manna' means 'what is it?'"

"Nu-uh, Dennie."

"Yes sir, Chris, Blake told me."

"The Nephites were the good guys," Chris argued. "You got it mixed up."

Dennie laughed. "The Nephites were the good guys in the Book of Mormon. The Israelites were the good guys in the Bible. I promise."

"Let's gather manna!" Chris yelled. He stretched the front of his Darth Vader shirt to form a bowl and raced through the parking lot loading handfuls of white petals onto Vader's face.

The next morning, Dennie and Chris met Ron and Tammy Babcock outside the temple. Bishop and Sister Babcock had come to witness Blake and Karin's sealing. After the adults went inside for the wedding, Ron and Dennie took Chris and Tammy to the visitors' center. Together, they admired the statue of Christ with his outstretched hands. Then, they walked hand in hand around the temple grounds while Chris and Tammy eyed coins in the fountain. Dennie was quiet that morning, inward. "A penny for your thoughts," Ron said.

"I was thinking about the last time we came here for baptisms. Aimy and Thes were with us."

"I haven't seen much of Aimy lately," Ron commented. "How is she?"

Dennie shrugged. "I haven't seen her much either. I've been busy helping Karin with the wedding. I'm worried about Aimy." Then Dennie told Ron that Aimy felt like a leftover person, someone left over in the pre-existence after Heavenly Father put all of the good families together. Dennie's brow furrowed as she told Ron of her own concerns. Were there leftover people? Were there people whose lives didn't really matter? She mentioned the mustangs they had seen at the Allens. They were rescued, but so many other horses were callously slaughtered, leftover life with no protection or purpose. Were some of Heavenly Father's children like that?

"You can't be a leftover person if someone cares about you," Ron said. "You can't be a leftover person if you help others. Jesus died for every single person. Nobody was left over. I think people are only left over if they choose to be, if they purposely hurt other people and knowingly turn their back on what's right. We have to help Aimy realize how important she is. Maybe that's why temple sealings are so important—so no one is left out or left over."

Dennie felt tears crowd in her eyes. "When Thes and I were little we came here. We were sealed to Mom and Dad. Thes should be here today. We should be celebrating his nineteenth birthday this month. Thes should have been getting ready for a mission. He should have been going through the temple for his endowment. How could he blow it like he did, Ron? How could he? How could he turn himself into a leftover person? How could he turn me into a liar? How could he hurt me so much? He screwed up everything. Sometimes I hate him, Ron! I hate him!"

"Dennie," Ron said, gripping her hand tightly, "you need to talk to your parents about Thes. You can't carry it all. My grandpa used to say that family secrets can eat families alive."

"I can't, Ron. You don't understand. Thinking Thes was a hero means so much to my parents. I can't take that away from them!" Ron looked away from Dennie at the temple.

"You haven't told anyone the things I told you? Have you?" Dennie's voice was urgent.

"No," Ron said. "Of course not."

Blake and Karin emerged from the temple. They beamed. Dennie wiped her eyes. Chris raced to them, burying his face in the fullness of his mother's wedding dress.

Later that evening, the wedding party arrived at the church an hour before the reception. The Relief Society president, who was helping with the food, ran out to meet them. "Karin," she exclaimed. "We just got here! The fish in the centerpieces are dead! What shall we do?"

Chris shrieked and pointed an accusing finger at his mother. "I told you I needed to help with them! The temperature of the water had to be right! They had to have their own seashells! You killed them!" Karin grabbed Chris's hand, but he broke away and ran.

Blake squeezed Karin's other hand. "How about if I find Chris and you figure out the decorations."

"OK," Karin said, suddenly dismal.

Dennie followed Karin into the bathroom. Karin started to sniffle. She kept dabbing at her mascara to keep it from smearing. "I do such stupid things, Dennie. What's wrong with me! Those little fish had feelings! Someday Blake will wonder why he married me!"

Meryl Fletcher came into the bathroom. Karin burst out, "Oh, Meryl, what are we going to do about the centerpieces? We can't have dead fish floating around."

"Next week we'll laugh about this, perhaps even tomorrow. I could send Rick to the pet store for more fish," Meryl suggested as she put her arm around Karin.

Karin shook her head. "I've killed enough fish for one day. Have you seen Chris?"

Meryl nodded. "He's calming down. That's why I came in to get Dennie. Chris wants her to help him bury the fish outside. Rick tried to convince him to flush them down the toilet. But he won't have it. Only a proper burial for fish with feelings."

Dennie went outside with Chris. They picked a spot on the side of the building, safe from the wind, where the bordering trees were still pregnant with blossoms. To dig a hole in the dirt, they used a spoon and a knife that Chris had swiped from the kitchen.

"Chris," Dennie said as they covered the fish bodies with soil. "Your mom feels really bad about what happened."

"I know she didn't mean it," Chris sighed. "Everything is going to change now that Blake and Mom are married. Blake says it will be a good change. It was a good change when the Israelites left Egypt. It was a good change when Han Solo met Luke Skywalker. Mom and Blake promised." Then, Chris stretched onto his tiptoes and cut a bunch of blossoms from the tree. He carefully placed them on the fish's graves. He looked up at Dennie. His eyes widened and a look of enlightenment crossed his smooth features. "Dennie, I have an idea," he said softly. "We could help Mom. These blossoms would look pretty in the fishbowls."

Dennie nodded and smiled in agreement. They formulated a plan. Dennie ran to her car and used the cell phone to call the bishop and ask his permission. She hustled into the church and secured her mother's approval. She took Karin and Blake into a classroom and insisted they wait in there for a surprise.

Then, Dennie and Meryl joined Chris outside and helped him finish cutting flowers from the trees. Back in the cultural hall, they filled the pretty, fluted-edged bowls with bunches of spring blossoms. Chris went into the classroom and blindfolded his mother and Blake with double-thick paper towels. He led them into the gym. "Manna from heaven," Chris announced as Karin and Blake Taylor lowered the blindfolds.

"The flowers are white like the lights on the trees," Karin beamed. "They're unique and perfect!" Then, Karin and her husband folded Chris in their arms.

CHAPTER 18

Our Only Hope

Thes made his debut as a football player with the Grantlin Junior Eagles when he was eleven years old. During the first half of the game, he played defense. His big break came at the beginning of the second quarter. Thes intercepted a pass, grabbing the ball out of the air. He raced up the field, ignoring defenders, oblivious to Dad running down the sideline yelling. With the ball safely tucked in the crook of his arm, he focused on the goal line, then beyond the goal line, on the clouds. Thes wasn't just playing football; he was racing the sky. People gasped! That kid! That little kid! Wow, could he run! No one could touch him! The only problem was my brother ran the wrong way that day. He had forgotten that the teams switched directions at the beginning of the quarter. He made a touchdown for the opposite team.

I remember Thes's huge grin, thinking he had scored. I remember Dad's moan. Adults laughed. Teammates yelled at him. When Thes realized what happened, his grin evaporated; he slammed the ball into the ground, his face deep red.

For the rest of his life, my brother played football with a vengeance, as if determined to score each time his fingers held the ball. He became a star. This past fall, Thes's senior year, Grantlin's varsity team seemed unbeatable. Games became community events. The town roared their approval. Thes Fletcher, the star running back, and Bryan Jones, the quarterback, were offensive heroes. Ty Edwards became known as the defensive menace. After winning every game during the regular season, their final championship game occurred in mid December. It was for the division title.

I remember that night. It was cold with a fog whose fingers reached through you. I hung out with some kids in the ward. Aimy and Brak sat apart from the crowd, wrapped together in a black-and-red plaid woolen blanket. Mom and Dad socialized with a group of adults. The town of Grantlin thundered with applause at the kickoff.

But the game was ugly from the beginning. Bryan was injured during the third possession. Thes was double-teamed by two of the best tackles in the division. Over and over they ground my brother into the turf. To make matters worse, our defense shut down. The other team scored three touchdowns before the half.

During halftime, Mom and Dad brought me hot chocolate and a blanket. Mom told me she'd spoken with Bryan's parents. They had checked on Bryan in the locker room. Bryan's shoulder was strained. He'd be out the rest of the game. Dad mentioned that our defense was as slow as molasses. "I hope Thes can break lose," Dad said. "He's our only hope."

"If there were a cloud to race, or stars," I said, "then he'd be in the end zone." Mom and Dad chuckled, remembering when Thes was little, the way he would race clouds and stars, on his bike, on foot, anywhere, always. What they didn't realize was that I was serious. If there were a hole in the sky where a star could shine through, if he could have focused on the sky for a moment, it might have given his legs wings. But the fog was thickening.

During the second half, Aimy stole a megaphone from someone in the band. She ran up and down the sidelines screaming encouragement to Thes. I remember her loose jeans, her leather jacket, and the way her white hair stood out even in the fog. The cheerleaders gazed down their noses at Aimy's antics. To them she was an idiot, an annoyance, an insect. Lisa Gibbons, a cheerleader who Thes occasionally dated, flipped her long cinnamon-colored hair. She literally fumed as she watched Aimy. Her stance was so angry that the fog could have been smoke coming out of her ears. She stalked over and swore at Aimy. Aimy ignored Lisa and screamed into the megaphone. Thes scored a touchdown. The crowd went wild with cheers. During the moment of celebration, Brak strode up to Aimy, grabbed her hand and jerked her out of the stadium.

Grantlin scored one more touchdown that night, but it wasn't enough to win the game. Brak and Aimy never came back. When I left the stadium, the blanket they had cuddled in was on the bleacher, lying in a crumpled heap. That night, Thes called from Ty's house and said he was spending the night. The next Monday at school, I heard Lisa teasing Thes about how funny he was when he was drunk.

The bell rang, dismissing the students in Gary Babcock's fourth-period Biology class. Only Aimy Tomlinson lingered in her seat. Aimy had missed the last two days of school. She hadn't been sick though. She didn't have that luxury. She had missed school because her mother was ill. Moni had been throwing up for two days with a raging migraine that pounded her brain. Aimy was exhausted. After coming home from work for the past three nights, she had curled up in a sleeping bag on her mother's bedroom floor. Last night, at four A.M., she had driven a frantic, suicidal Moni to the emergency room and begged the doctor to give her mother a shot to make her sleep, to kill the pain.

The bedraggled emergency-room doctor recognized Moni Tomlinson. She had been in here before. Too many times. When her name was entered into the computer there were red flags everywhere documenting a history of prescription drug abuse and chemical dependency. The woman needed rehabilitation and counseling, not a shot to deaden the pain. Then the doctor looked at the elf-like girl with her. The child was visibly worn out. She was about the same age as the doctor's son. But the girl's blue eyes looked old tonight, with the dark bags under them betraying her utter weariness. The doctor gave the woman a shot so the girl could rest.

After the shot, Aimy drove a limp Moni home and put her to bed. She snatched two hours of sleep, then dressed and went to school. She would never catch up in her classes. *I don't care,* she told herself as she blinked furiously to keep her eyes open. But she did care. For some reason, she couldn't stand the thought of disappointing Mr. Babcock, Bishop Babcock.

"Aimy, have you been sick?" Mr. Babcock walked over to her desk after the rest of the class left.

Aimy nodded. "I was wondering if I could hang out here during lunch and catch up on my lab notebook."

"Sure," he said. "I'm going over to the teacher's lounge to get something to eat. I'll be back in about ten minutes. Can I get you something?"

"No thanks. I brought a sandwich," Aimy lied. She had a bruised apple in her backpack. It would hold her until she went to work at three-thirty.

Aimy took out her lab notebook and colored pencils. She began constructing careful illustrations of mitochondria and chloroplasts. The classroom door opened and Brak Meyers walked in. Aimy's heart skipped a beat. She looked up at him warily, thinking of how she hadn't talked to him since the day after he received her letter. "You don't mean it, Aimy," he had said that day. "You'll be back. We're meant for each other." But she hadn't been back. She would never go back, not after how he had threatened Dennie. She had made a decision. She wasn't going to make the same mistakes as her mother.

"Hi," Brak said. Aimy nodded shortly.

"Long time, no see," Brak said as he walked over to a glass cupboard. He stood there as he spoke, studying Mr. Babcock's collection of chemicals. "I hear you've been seeing Ron Babcock. Mr. Babcock usually doesn't let people hang out in his lab during lunch. Since you're dating a family member, I guess you get special privileges."

"I haven't been seeing Ron Babcock. Ron likes Dennie."

"Don't lie to me, Aimy! I saw him bring you home Saturday night!"

"There were other people in the car. It was a family thing."

"You don't have a family." Brak looked through the cupboard and took a vial out. "HCL, hydrochloric acid, a strong acid with the ionization content of ten to the seventh. Aimy, you hurt me. What do you think would happen if I poured some of this on your cheek? I wonder what the burn would look like? Maybe, then, I wouldn't want you so much."

Brak began walking toward Aimy. She stood up and backed away. "Mr. Babcock's going to be back any minute."

Brak poured acid on Aimy's lab notebook, destroying the illustration she had been working on. Aimy turned to run, but Brak was quicker and stronger. She felt his grip tear into her arm.

Gary Babcock heard the scream on his way towards his classroom. He ran. Before gaining the door, he saw Aimy through the window, backed into a corner, one arm shielding her face. Brak Meyers was shouting at her, with a vial of some chemical in his outstretched hand and cold hatred in his eyes.

Bishop Babcock threw the door open and flung himself into the side of the boy. The vial flew from Brak's hand as the man's weight crushed him. Bishop Babcock's glasses clattered to the floor. "Aimy,"

Gary Babcock gasped, "push the red button next to the phone." Sobbing, Aimy ran and pushed the emergency alarm.

Bishop Gary Babcock twisted Brak's arm behind his back and spoke through clenched teeth to the boy pinned beneath him. "She's God's child! Do you understand that? She's not yours to threaten or harm! Do you understand? She's God's child!"

Two security guards burst into the room. "It's OK, man, we're here," said one as he helped Mr. Babcock up. The other handcuffed Brak and led him from the room. On his way out, Brak turned to Aimy. "I wouldn't have hurt you! I just wanted you to know how I felt. I love you."

Aimy sat in a chair shivering. Bishop Babcock picked up his glasses and put them back on. He went to the sink where he filled a paper cup with water.

"We have a couple of minutes," he said gently as he gave Aimy the drink of water. "Then we need to go to the office and tell the police what happened. Are you up to it?"

Aimy's voice was small as tears streamed down her face. "It's acid," Aimy cried, pointing to the broken vial and the liquid on the floor. She took a drink of water and set the cup on her desk. "Bishop, he was going to hurt me! Why didn't I know he was bad from the start? Why did I ever think he was good? I'm like my mom. I'm just like my mom."

Gary Babcock lowered himself into a chair facing Aimy. He took both of the girl's hands in his. "Aimy, honey, there's good and bad in all of us. Tenderness and meanness. But what you have to do is find the good and hold onto it. Brak didn't. He let go of it. But you and me, we must hold onto the good, with both hands, every single day of our lives. That's what Heavenly Father expects from us. That's our only hope. That's what defines who we are. That's what makes our lives worth something."

CHAPTER 19

Trust

I found a list the other day when I was going through a box of stuff I saved from junior high. Aimy and I had written down what we imagined people would be when they grew up. The list went like this: Aimy Tomlinson—actress. Dennie Fletcher—veterinarian. Kay Sherlock—singer of grocery-store melodies for commercials. Thomas Mcfinnigin—puffy-haired college professor. Jason Jutt—politician or prisoner of war. Thes Fletcher—pilot or paramedic.

Thes Fletcher—pilot or paramedic. I looked at Thes's name for a long time. I had picked pilot because of the way he loved to race the sky. Aimy had picked paramedic because she saw Thes as someone who rescued people. In five days it will be March 21, the spring equinox, the day we would have celebrated Thes's nineteenth birthday. I can't get over the feeling that he's missing out on the rest of his life. Theseus Lautaro Fletcher will never fly in a jet airplane or rescue anyone again.

But why didn't somebody rescue him? Like Bishop Babcock rescued Aimy. Thes held my hand when we ran away. He fed me. He protected me. He made sure Uncle Blake brought me to the United States. He hid Aimy. He pulled Chris out of the water. When did everything become a lie? Why didn't Heavenly Father rescue my brother? Why didn't I?

On Sunday, following the three-hour block of meetings, Bishop Babcock sat in the bishop's office. His first interview was with Dennie Fletcher. As he waited, his thoughts wandered. Now that Brak Meyers's parents had shipped him off to a reform facility, Bishop Babcock felt at ease as far as Aimy's safety went. He thanked the Lord once more for the feeling that prompted him to return to his classroom quickly that day.

But the bishop was concerned about Dennie. Two weeks ago, his little girl, Tammy, had come to him and recounted a conversation between Dennie and Ron that the child had overheard on the way home from the snowshoeing trip. Apparently, Ron and Dennie thought Tammy was sleeping. Tammy had begged her father not to tell Ron how she had listened. She was afraid that Ron and Dennie would never forgive her.

Initially, the bishop had wondered if Tammy dreamed up much of her tale. His youngest daughter had a vivid imagination. But, when she mentioned the names Brak and Ty, and when Tammy described boys drinking and spoke of lies surrounding Thes Fletcher's death, the bishop became deeply troubled.

It seemed ironic that this information surfaced right when the Fletchers were beginning to see light at the end of their tunnel of grief. Even in his sorrow, Rick Fletcher was proud of his son's heroism. The whole Fletcher family had felt joy in Blake Taylor and Karin Parker's union. Should the bishop stir up waters that were beginning to calm?

But if he were in the Fletchers' shoes, wouldn't he want to know exactly what happened? Wouldn't he want to know the truth about his son's life and death? The answer was a resounding *yes*—especially if it would help Dennie cope. What a heavy burden Dennie bore, if she bore it alone! The bishop pictured the Fletcher's family structure like a house that had been ripped apart by lightning at Theseus's death. There were three, not four, left to rebuild it. It had to be rebuilt on a foundation of truth.

Gary Babcock's thoughts strayed to a few evenings ago when he had tried to talk to Ron about Thes Fletcher and the events surrounding his drowning. But the discussion had been fruitless. "Anything Dennie has told me, she's told me in confidence," Ron had snapped. No one understood the importance of confidentiality better than Bishop Babcock. But members of his family, members of the ward were supposed to *confide* in him, *not* keep confidences from him.

The bishop's thoughts were interrupted a moment later, when Dennie walked into the office. He shook her hand. She had such dark eyes, deep and lovely. But those eyes held too many secrets and too much hurt. The child needed to leave those burdens at the Lord's feet. The bishop felt it. He knew it.

They visited for five minutes as if it were a normal semi-annual Bishop-Laurel interview. The bishop asked routine questions; Dennie gave the routine answers. Then Bishop Babcock took a silent breath and continued. "Dennie, there are some difficult questions I need to ask you. Some things we must talk about." As Bishop Babcock spoke, Dennie's silence became like thick smoke between them, clogging her throat and stinging her eyes. "Did Thes have a drinking problem?" A tiny nod. "Were your parents aware of this?" A barely perceptible shake of the head. "Did Thes's drinking have anything to do with his death?"

"I can't talk anymore. I can't," Dennie finally whispered. Then, she fled. Ron, who had been waiting outside to offer her a ride home, tried to stop her. "What's wrong Dennie?" he asked.

"You promised," she gulped. "I trusted you." Then, she ran from the building. Instead of following her, Ron turned towards his father's office as a storm rose within him. As Gary Babcock's irate son burst through the door, a feeling of helplessness seeped into the bishop's heart like lead.

As Sean Garrett put on his overalls in a back room of Beef Burgers, he felt vaguely disillusioned with his life. It was Sunday. He didn't like working on Sundays. Should he go to college? Get another job? This job was OK. After all, he was assistant manager. But it would be nice to have a job that paid enough to get him out of the dingy apartment he was renting, that was stable enough to eventually support a family. Plus, he was sick and tired of answering to Owen. He was a better manager than Owen and he knew it.

To make matters worse, he hadn't gone on a date since he had gotten home from his mission three months ago. He needed to start dating, to find someone whom he could eventually marry. But most of all, he needed to get Aimy Tomlinson off his mind. Not that she was the little pixie girl he remembered from before his mission. Not now! She was far from that! But she was still too young, too tough, too independent, too vulnerable, way too young. Yet, something about her tugged at his heart.

Take just yesterday when he heard that Aimy's ex-boyfriend had attacked her in the science lab. If Bishop Babcock hadn't happened along, the jerk would have maimed her. When Sean found out, his heart had skipped a beat, then pounded ferociously. He wanted to plant a fist in the kid's face and lock him up for time and all eternity. It wasn't a very Christlike attitude for a returned missionary.

Sean looked at the clock. Aimy's shift should have started twenty minutes ago. He would have to chew her out when she came in. Sean took a deep breath. He definitely needed to get his mind and his heart off of Aimy Tomlinson.

The telephone rang. He picked it up. "Beef Burgers."

Sean knew something was wrong the instant he heard the pitch of Aimy's voice. "Sean-nee, I can't come to work today. Please don't let Owen fire me. Please."

"What's wrong?"

She hesitated. "I gotta go."

"Are you home? Do you need help?"

She was already gone. As Sean put the phone on the receiver, he had the urge to drive to her house at that moment. He looked over the restaurant. He was down an employee and customers were pouring in. There was nothing he could do. Not right now, anyway.

Dennie walked and ran the two miles home from the church. She had taken her heels off. The ground was so cold. Holes tore in her nylons. Tears stung her eyes. She covered her mouth with her hand and bit her lower lip. Why had Ron violated her trust? How could he? Ron was like Ty. A liar. He had callously hurt her, the person he was supposed to care about. That was the kind of thing Brak did, not Ron! Did he think it would help her? How could he lie and hurt her like that? Did everyone do that? Lie and hurt the people they suppos-edly loved?

Dennie neared her home. She couldn't go in. Her parents were there. How long would it be before the bishop called them in for interviews? Before his words tore off the thin scab covering the tear in their hearts? She couldn't look into their eyes. She had hidden too much from them.

Dennie gazed at the bedraggled house across the street. Why

hadn't Aimy come to church today? Yet she knew Aimy would be there for her. You aren't a leftover person if someone cares about you, and you care about each other. Dennie walked to the front door. She heard Aimy's panic-ridden voice inside.

"Moni wake up! Please!"

Dennie opened the door without knocking. Moni lay limply on the coach with Aimy beside her, shaking her. "Mommy, please, Mommy wake up!"

"Aimy, what happened?" Dennie ran to them.

"I can't wake her up, Dennie! I can't wake her up!"

"Why? Did she fall? Did she take something?"

"She's always taking pills! She could have taken anything. Tranquilizers, pain medicine, alcohol. I don't know!"

"We have to call an ambulance," Dennie said.

"No!" Aimy grabbed Dennie's hand and placed Dennie's fingers on Moni's wrist. "See, she has a pulse! Her heart's beating. The drugs just have to wear off! She'll be OK. She has to be OK."

"Aimy, we have to call! Moni could die!"

"Not yet! She'll wake up in a minute. If we call, they'll take her to the hospital. They'll lock her up. Moni's not strong enough. It'll kill her. They'll send me to live with my grandmother in Texas or put me in some foster home. She's all I have, Dennie." Aimy dug her nails into Dennie's arm and looked in her eyes. "Den, you're my best friend. I know you understand. I know you'll help me. Moni will be OK. I can't lose her. I don't want to be alone!"

"I need to go to the bathroom," Dennie said. She left Aimy with her mother and walked through the kitchen. There was a hot dog boiling in a pan on the stove. Aimy must have put it on for lunch. Dennie thought of how white and chilled Moni's hand had felt in hers. She thought of Thes. Dennie picked up the cordless telephone, took it into the bathroom where Aimy could not hear, and dialed 911.

Dennie brought Aimy a glass of water and sat down beside her. When Aimy heard the sound of sirens careening towards her house, she looked at Dennie in disbelief. "Dennie, you didn't! You couldn't! I trusted you!" Then she put her head on her mother's chest and wept.

CHAPTER 20

The Right Thing

Dennie stood dizzily on the edge of the events whirling around her. Paramedics worked on Moni. Her parents materialized. Sean Garrett showed up. A firefighter questioned Dennie about Moni's conditon. Dennie shook her head and answered, "I just got here. I don't know what happened. I think she took too much medicine or something."

Moni was loaded on a stretcher and hooked up to some kind of moniter. Aimy watched, pale, numb, and shivering. "Will my mom be OK?" Aimy questioned a female firefighter.

"I hope so. Come on. You can ride with me to the hospital." The firefighter put a blanket around Aimy and led her to the truck. Dennie ran over to Aimy and offered to meet her at the hospital. "Stay away," Aimy said with agony in her eyes as she climbed into the emergency vehicle.

The sirens of the fire truck, police car, and ambulance rang through the neighborhood once more, leaving behind the quiet of a cool Sunday afternoon, a few birds rustling in a tree, and the smell of Aimy's hot dog burning on the stove. Sean raced into the kitchen and turned off the burner. He put the pan in the sink and turned on cold water. The hot dog sizzled as it cooled. White steam rose.

Sean went back out into the front room and spoke to the Fletchers. "I'll go to the hospital and wait with Aimy. Y'all go home. I'll call you when I know something."

"Thanks, Sean," Rick Fletcher shook the young man's hand. "Tell Aimy that our prayers are with her and her mother."

After Sean left, Dennie's parents turned toward her with a barrage of questions. What happened to Moni? Was it an overdose of drugs? Medications? Alcohol? Why are you here? Are you all right?

"I stopped to see Aimy after my interview with the bishop," Dennie answered awkwardly. "Moni was unconscious and Aimy was trying to wake her up. She didn't know for sure what was wrong with her mom, except that Moni's always taking stuff. Aimy didn't want me to call the ambulance. She said the drugs just needed to wear off. She's scared that Moni will be institutionalized. Aimy thinks that she'll be put in some foster home or sent to relatives in Texas. She thinks I took away her only family."

"You did the right thing," her mother reassured her. "Aimy will see that."

Dennie shook her head and whispered, "Mama, sometimes there isn't a right thing."

"But this time there was," her father stepped to her other side. "You called the ambulance because you knew Moni was in danger. You had to help her even if it meant losing Aimy's friendship. That was taking a risk. It's like when Thes saved Ty. It cost him his life, but he took the risk, he did the right thing."

Dennie backed away from her parents. "NO, DAD, NO!" She covered her face with her hands. She bit her lip so hard she tasted the blood.

"Dennie, what is it?" Her mother's voice seemed to drown out the sound of the birds outside.

A sickness enveloped Dennie. She looked at the people who loved her and her voice was like the wind roaring in her ears. "Thes didn't die trying to save Ty. He was drunk. He fell into the ocean. It's a lie. It's all a lie! I LIED, MOM AND DAD! I LIED!"

They didn't crumble. They didn't fall sobbing to the floor. They didn't strike out at her. They just stared at her, the look in their eyes screaming, "This can't be our Dennie! This can't be our Dennie!"

Dennie walked out of Aimy's house and no one stopped her. She walked across the street. She found her keys in her purse. She got into the Tahoe that was parked in the driveway and drove away.

She drove to Ty Edwards's house. She rang the doorbell. She stood there in her church dress, shoeless, with holes in her nylons. Blood reddened her lips and mascara stained her cheeks. She hated Ty. She hated him even more than she hated Brak. Part of her wanted to destroy him. But, since she could not, she wanted him to know how he had destroyed her and her family.

Mrs. Edwards answered the door. "Is Ty home?" Dennie asked.

Mrs. Edwards stared at her. She knew who Dennie was. But she couldn't imagine why the girl stood on her front step, disheveled, with thick, cold eyes, on a Sunday afternoon. A tremor of anxiety passed through her. She had never forgotten the fear when the coast guard called and said there had been an accident, nor the feeling that came over her when he explained that Ty was fine; it was Thes Fletcher who was gone. Alice Edwards still felt guilty about that surge of joyous relief. Today, the dead boy's sister stood in front of her like a dark phantom of her guilt, an image from a nightmare.

Mr. Edwards glimpsed Dennie from the family room where he was watching TV. He turned off the television. "Ty, someone's here for you," he yelled down the hall. He invited Dennie to have a seat in the living room. Dennie sat down stiffly. Mr. and Mrs. Edwards sat down next to each other on the couch. Mr. Edwards put his arm around his wife.

Ty came in. He wore jeans and a maroon pullover sweater. "Dennie," he said.

"I told my parents," Dennie said. "They know you lied about Thes's death. They know what really happened." Ty sank heavily into a chair.

Mrs. Edwards interrupted. "Dennie, we're sorry Thes is gone. We know you are hurting. But Ty wouldn't lie about something like that."

"My brother was drunk! It's Ty's fault! Thes and Ty were drinking buddies! Thes fell into the ocean!"

"Dennie, please leave," Mrs. Edwards began. Ty raised his hand, stopping his mother. "No, Mom. Dennie, it wasn't like you think." Ty closed his eyes as if he wanted to shut out the world. The doorbell rang. Mr. Edwards answered the door and led Meryl and Rick Fletcher into the room.

"We were looking for Dennie," Rick Fletcher said uncomfortably. "We saw the car parked outside."

"Perhaps it would be best if you took Dennie home," Mrs. Edwards said painfully.

"Alice," her husband interrupted. "Let Ty choreograph this."

"I need to talk to all of you." Ty said slowly. Mr. Edwards brought in chairs from the kitchen for the Fletchers. The group waited like statues for Ty to begin.

CHAPTER 21

The Beating of One Heart

The group in Alice Edwards's living room sat in a semi-circle, facing each other—similar to the configuration Alice set up in her living room when her friends came over for their monthly committee meetings. Alice noticed that Meryl Fletcher looked pale, but before sitting down Meryl had squeezed her daughter's hand. Rick Fletcher's jaw was bunched and his brow was furrowed. Were his emotions like lava in a volcano? Would they erupt and burn her son?

"Ty has something to say. He's not perfect, but he's our son and we love him. We'd ask that you hear him out," Mr. Edwards said as he began the conversation.

Ty looked at the floor as he spoke, "I lied about my buddy's death." Then he looked up at Dennie, his hazel eyes meeting the darkness of her stare. "Dennie, I didn't lie for the same reasons that Marlow did in the *Heart of Darkness*. I didn't lie because I was afraid your family couldn't handle what really happened. I lied because if . . . I don't know how to say it. I lied because it just came out that way when the police asked me so many questions and maybe it was easier answering them that way. Less complicated. But it wasn't just that. It was partly because I wanted the world to understand the kind of guy Thes was. It was like—I knew that if I had fallen into the ocean . . ." Ty stopped and took a breath. Would that accusing look ever leave Dennie's eyes? Would she always hate him?

"I tried to tell you what happened, Dennie!" he burst. "But you wouldn't let me! I knew Thes would have wanted you to know the truth. Then, you could decide whether or not your parents needed to know. Thes didn't die like you think, Dennie. Brak lied too."

Ty was quiet for a moment as if the confession had exhausted him. Dennie felt as if she had been turned to stone. Her heart was a lump of granite and her dry eyes stared straight ahead without blinking, without believing.

Meryl Fletcher reached across the space between the chairs and touched Ty's knee. "Ty, please tell me what happened to my son."

Ty looked up at the ceiling as his thoughts reached like groping hands for words to describe the past. "Over a year ago, I went with Thes to a party after a game. I gave him his first drink. I had heard that some people become alcoholics after one drink, like they have a weakness for the disease. But I didn't believe it. I had never seen it. Mr. and Mrs. Fletcher, I didn't know what alcohol would do to Thes, how he would use it to wipe out pain. How he couldn't control it. How it controlled him.

"First, I told myself he was just a guy getting drunk. But then it got worse. He had to have something to drink everyday. Sometimes, he would drink until he passed out. I knew he needed to stop, but I didn't know how to stop him. We both were good at keeping things hidden from our parents. Once, I talked to our priest about it. Finally, I decided that the best I could do was to become my brother's keeper. *I* stopped drinking. If I couldn't get Thes to quit at least I could keep him safe. I could make sure he didn't drive.

"Sometimes Thes wanted to stop. He even told me that he had promised Dennie. I tried to talk him into getting some help. But he still brought a six pack to the ocean *that* day. We argued most of the way there. I told him if he wanted to poison himself, he'd have to do it in someone else's car. He didn't open any of the cans. He was really quiet and I could tell he was thinking, trying to make some kind of decision. Then when we got to Salt Point, Thes took the beer cans out of the car. He opened them up and poured the stuff down the rocks, watching it sizzle into the ocean. He told me he had quit. Then, he wanted to get out on the rocks as fast as he could to fish. We picked up the beer cans and walked back to the car to get our fishing gear.

"That's when Brak Meyers showed up in the parking lot. He hated Thes. He really hated him. He yelled some obscenities at us. We ignored him and went out to fish. We weren't afraid of Brak. There were two of us. We knew we could finish Brak off if we wanted to. We walked out on the rocks as far as we could. Meyers didn't follow us. We started fishing. We thought Meyers was gone.

"It was windy and clear that day. The water was really rough. We were catching fish. A few hours passed. The tide rose. The waves were savage. Over and over again I told Thes that it was time to go. But he wouldn't come in. He kept saying that he wanted to stay a little longer, to catch another fish. Finally, I told him I was going in. He turned to me and asked me to take in the two buckets of fish. He said he'd bring the poles and the bait in a few minutes. My pole was about six feet away from Thes wedged between two rocks. I started back, but Thes just kept fishing. It was like he never wanted to stop. Like he didn't want to go back to the real world.

"I climbed back towards the bluffs. That's when I saw Brak. He was making his way toward Thes. Meyers picked up my pole. There was leftover bait on it. I don't know what Brak said to Thes. I couldn't hear them, but Brak fingered the bait like he was studying it. Waves were breaking all around them. Thes started getting his stuff together to come in. I started towards them. I didn't want Thes to have any trouble with Meyers.

"Then, Brak did the strangest thing. He cast my line up to a higher rock where there were a bunch of seagulls. A gull grabbed the piece of squid on the hook. The bird took off with the hook in his mouth. Meyers let out a little more line. The gull beat its wings frantically, unable to fly away.

"Thes was mad. He put his bamboo rod down and grabbed the pole from Brak. The ocean kept rising. I yelled for Thes to come in. The waves scared Brak. He climbed up to a higher rock. But Thes stayed where he was. He started to pull the line in, pulling the seagull slowly towards him. By this time I was on a ridge just above Thes.

"Cut the line!" I screamed. "Get out of there."

"The bird won't be able to eat with a hook in its mouth! It'll die!" Thes shouted back. An instant later he had the gull in his arms. It struggled and pecked at him. Its eyes were wild. He knelt down on the rock to hold the bird steady. His knees were in the foam. He was so focused on freeing the gull in his arms that he didn't see the wave rising. I shouted, but if he heard me, he didn't show it.

"He worked the hook out, then he opened his arms and the gull lifted into the air. That's when it hit. When the wave receded, Thes was gone. For a moment I saw him struggling in the water. Brak grabbed me. He pushed me against a rock. He yelled that there was nothing anybody could do. He said I'd be dead if I went into that water. He was crying and I listened to him. He pulled me back to the bluff. He asked for my keys. He brought me my car phone. 'Call 911,' he said. 'Don't tell anyone I was here. I didn't mean for this to happen. I saved your life.' Then Meyers left. I called the police.

"While I waited, I screamed at the waves. I called to Thes. I prayed. I tried to make bargains with God. I said the opening verses of mass over and over again. *I will go unto the altar of God. Unto God, who giveth joy to my youth.* I knew if we had switched places, if I had been in the water, Thes would have gone into the ocean after me. Brak couldn't have stopped him. When the police came, I told them the lie. I'm sorry. I'm so sorry."

The sound of Ty's ragged breathing filled the room. His face was wet with tears. Rick Fletcher was the first to speak. His head was bowed and his words were filled with pain. "Ty, I don't blame you. I wasn't always a good father to Thes. I was too critical. Too angry. Maybe things would have been different if I were different. Maybe he would have wanted to come home earlier that day if he felt more accepted. Maybe he would have talked to me about his problems."

Meryl Fletcher grabbed her husband's hand and spoke through tears. "Rick, I never listened to you when you felt like something was really wrong with Thes. I should have known Thes was hurting, that he was in trouble. I kept telling myself that things were OK. He just had to get through his teen years. I should have noticed that things weren't right."

"Don't you get it!" Dennie screamed, "I KNEW! I knew all along! I saw Thes with the beer in the car! If I had told you earlier, you would have gotten him help! If I told you that day, you wouldn't have let him go! It's my fault!! I killed my brother!!"

"No!" Her parents shouted in unison. They ran to her. They held her fiercely in their arms and their bodies shook with her sobs. It was as if there was nothing between them, and their grief rose like the beating of the same heart.

CHAPTER 22

Racing the Sky

Dennie heard the telephone ring while she and her parents sat at the kitchen table eating a light dinner of soup and sandwiches. The meal was quiet and no one was very hungry. Meryl Fletcher picked up the phone on its third ring. Dennie could tell that Sean Garrett was calling from the hospital.

A chill went through Dennie. She hoped Moni was OK. Her mother hung up the phone and related the conversation. "Moni is still in serious condition, but she has regained consciousness. Tomorrow the doctors plan to run additional tests to determine the extent of damage the drugs have done to her organs. Aimy is going to spend the night in the hospital lobby." Dennie's heart ached. It physically hurt. Now that her parents knew the truth, it felt almost as if she had had surgery and that portions of guilt and fear had been cut out of her.

It left her exhausted and aching. She ached for herself. She ached for her parents. To them, Thes had died all over again this afternoon. And she hurt for Aimy. When she thought of her friend, a cloud of helplessness threatened to engulf her. "I wish we could do something," she whispered.

Rick Fletcher, who had been pale and silent since they had come home from the Edwards, spoke. "Then let's do something. Let's go to the hospital."

"But Dad, Aimy told me to stay away," Dennie said painfully.

"She'll know we cared enough to come," he said.

"I think we should go," Meryl added. "We love Aimy. At the very least we could tell her that." Dennie nodded.

When they arrived at the hospital, they found Sean Garrett and Bishop Babcock in a small foyer near the nurses' station. Bishop Babcock's face was lined with fatigue, betraying the fact that it had been an incredibly difficult Sunday for him. He shook Meryl and Rick Fletcher's hands. Sean hugged Dennie. After Sean's hug, the bishop, almost nervously, extended his hand toward Dennie. Was he afraid she might bolt? But she didn't. She shook her bishop's hand.

"Hi Dennie," he said gently, not mentioning their conversation earlier in the day. Dennie wondered if he realized that to her the interview seemed to have taken place a lifetime ago. The bishop continued, "Dennie, Moni's asleep now. It's a good time to speak with Aimy. To bless her life with your friendship once more." *But what if Aimy didn't want Dennie's friendship anymore?* She had to try though. She could at least let Aimy know she was there. She could at least tell Aimy she loved her.

Dennie stood cautiously outside the hospital room. She gazed in. Moni looked pale and childlike in the hospital bed. She was hooked up to tubes that both monitored and sustained her life. Aimy sat on a chair beside Moni's bed with her eyes glassily fixed on a television near the ceiling. The TV program was running but the sound had been turned off. Dennie cleared her throat and stepped into the room. Aimy looked up.

"Hi," Dennie said.

"Density," Aimy returned. It was enough of an invitation for Dennie to pull a chair next to her friend and sit down. Without talking, they watched *Xena, Warrior Princess,* in a seemingly silent pantomime, disarm a hoard of monstrous men. When Xena had wiped her sword clean and was grinning victoriously, Aimy picked up the remote control and turned off the television.

"How's Moni?" Dennie asked.

"She's really sick. The doctor said Mom could have died today. They are going to keep her in the hospital until she's through withdrawal. Then, they will send her to a rehab clinic. I'm scared Density. I don't know what's going to happen." Aimy clenched her fists.

"You can stay at my house until Moni gets better," Dennie offered.

"I won't need to. Bishop Babcock called my Aunt Joni in Texas. She's flying in tomorrow. I've only met her a couple of times. I guess she's going to be my babysitter."

A long moment of silence passed. "Aimy, I had to call," Dennie said desperately. "I kept thinking how Thes might have lived if I had done things differently."

"It's OK," Aimy said softly. "It's not your fault that leftover people live across the street from you."

Dennie took her friend's hand. "Aimy, you aren't a leftover person! You can't be a leftover person if Jesus died for you! You can't be a leftover person if someone loves you! I love you."

Aimy began to cry. "I love her, Dennie. I love my mom."

"I know," Dennie said, and even though her own soul felt desperately tired, she cradled her sobbing friend in her arms.

Later that night, the Fletchers brought Aimy home with them. Dennie gave Aimy her bed and slept on the floor. Dennie awakened at four in the morning. She thought of how Thes used to be afraid of all the rooms and all of the ghosts. Dennie looked at Aimy fast asleep, her hair disheveled and her features softened by the darkness.

Dennie walked soundlessly into Thes's room. She opened his blinds and looked at the stars. She thought again of how Thes was afraid of ghosts. She knelt by Thes's bed and cradled his pillow in her arms. Then, for the first time in a long time, Dennie opened her whole soul to her Father in Heaven. She prayed for Aimy and Moni, for Thes, for herself, and for her parents. No light filled the room. Her brother did not come to her in a vision. But in the darkness she felt the ache inside her ease a bit. And when she went back into her room, she slept soundly without being troubled by dreams.

On Monday afternoon, Dennie and Aimy were at the airport waiting for Aunt Joni's plane to disembark. "Dennie, how will we recognize her?" Aimy said worriedly. "She doesn't look anything like my mom, except that they both have green eyes."

They needn't have worried though, for Joni Evans, a short heavy woman in her early forties, had a picture of her niece, her little Cutie Bug, gripped tightly in her fist as she gathered her things and readied herself to leave the airplane. She had cared for little Aimy for the first two years of her life while her kid sister, Moni, had gone to beauty school, and then started her first job. What a demanding fireball that baby had been! Just like Joni when she was little. Then Moni had up

and moved to California, and Joni's arms had longed for her Cutie
Bug. Joni shoved the picture into her large canvas purse. She didn't
need the picture. She stepped off the plane. She felt certain that she
would recognize Cutie Bug anywhere.

And she did! There was her little Aimy standing next to a pretty,
dark-haired girl. That must be Dennie, the neighbor, Joni thought.
Lands! People give their kids the strangest names! What a skinny
thing Cutie Bug's turned into! Joni broke into a run. She threw her
arms around her niece and fell into a ferocious barrage of tears. When
she was able to step back and get a closer look at Aimy, she sniffled
and swiped at her eyes with her sleeve. Her voice boomed out,
"Lands, Cutie Bug, you're so skinny! You're guaranteed to gain ten
pounds 'fore I'm done with you!"

At eight o'clock that same evening, the Fletcher's doorbell rang.
Dennie answered it. Ron Babcock and his Doberman, Gretchen,
stood on the porch.

"Hey," Dennie greeted him self-consciously. She hadn't spoken to
him since that awful moment on Sunday.

"Hey," Ron returned. Then, he shifted his weight, cleared his
throat and sang rather nervously. "You are a lady and I'm an old sock.
But I was just wondering, if you'd come for a walk."

Dennie reached down and stroked Gretchen. She really liked that
dog. She really liked Ron too. She sang softly with her eyes on the
Doberman, "You are a great guy and I am a clod. I hope you'll forgive
me for being a snob." Then, she looked up at Ron.

"Come on, you clod, Old Sock wants to talk," Ron grinned and
reached for Dennie's hand. Dennie could have sworn that Gretchen
was smiling too.

Later that night, Meryl Fletcher lay down on the bed next to her
teenage daughter. For a brief moment, she wished Dennie were a little
girl again. She missed the way Dennie's five-year-old head had fit
perfectly into the curve of her arm. Did Dennie feel as tired as she
did, so tired that even the muscles in her face felt like they sagged
from the weight of gravity? The blinds were open and a half-disc of
moon lighted the sky.

"Mom, do you remember how Thes slept with his blinds pulled all the way up so there was only glass between him and the lights outside? He was afraid of the dark so he would watch the moon and the stars until he fell asleep."

"I remember. After he was asleep, I used to come in and close his blinds so that the sun wouldn't wake him up too early. He could be ornery if he didn't get enough sleep."

"You're right," Dennie returned. Then she asked her mother a troubling question. "Do you think Thes blew it Mom, do you think he ruined his chance to be with our family forever? When he started drinking, he broke his baptismal covenants."

Dennie's father entered the room as Meryl Fletcher attempted to answer her daughter's question. "Oh, Dennie, I believe we have a loving Heavenly Father and a Savior who died so that everything will be right in the end. I believe that our family was sealed together forever in the temple around God's holy altar. I believe that my son's earthly life and his eternal life are of infinite worth to our Heavenly Father. I believe with all my being that we will be with Thes again."

"What I can't stop thinking about," Rick Fletcher spoke quietly. His brow was knit together and his Adam's apple convulsed as he swallowed. "What haunts me is that Thes thought a bird's life was more important than his own."

"No, Daddy," Dennie responded. "It's just that when Thes had a purpose, his whole energy and being focused on that one thing. Nothing else mattered to Thes at moments like that. That's what happened when Thes freed the bird. That's how Thes was."

"That's how Thes is," Meryl Fletcher gently corrected. "Dennie, Rick, no one lives perfectly. One day at the cancer center, before one of my radiation treatments, I was sitting in the waiting room with a man whom I had never seen before. He didn't have a shirt on and his emaciated torso was covered with tattoos. He was sweating profusely. He wore a filthy, tattered fisherman's hat and an angry scowl. At first glance, he seemed like a worthless, dying scrap of humanity.

"He began talking bitterly. 'I don't have to be here,' he said. 'I'm going to die anyway, you know. I don't have to have the treatment if I don't want it.' He swore and ranted about how he didn't have to do this. He had only agreed to the radiation because it might help him to make it to Southern California where he would rather die.

"I was feeling helpless and moody that day too. I mentioned how I was tired of the treatments. The doctors never knew for sure whether they would work. With cancer there were never any guarantees. I told this man that I was sick of it too.

"Then, Dennie, this human being whose life seemed so completely bitter, wasted, and even worthless said something to me, something I'll never forget. He looked at me through those defeated, blood-tinged eyes and spoke earnestly, saying, 'You have the rest of your life to live. You are still young. You have a family. You must finish the treatments and get well. And live.'

"I looked up at him and I saw something I had never seen before. I saw the image of God in his soul. I saw the Savior's compassion. With those words of loving concern for me, it was as if his whole countenance changed and I knew him as his Father in Heaven's child.

"Thes, too, is God's son. His last act on earth was loving and gentle. I believe, I *know,* that at his death, God claimed his life. But I miss him so much." Meryl Fletcher's voice broke. Rick and Dennie wept soundlessly. Then Meryl sat up and took her husband and daughter's hands. "My darlings," she said with strength in her voice that echoed her son's fierce courage. "We will trust our Heavenly Father and our Savior. We will go on and live."

When my Mama in Chile named me Mina, was she thinking of the darkness of a mine? Did she imagine the maze of tunnels, the danger of lamps failing and passageways collapsing, the multiple levels, the varying depths of shadows? Did she wonder if I would be trapped in the dark tunnels of my own soul? But, Mina also means source of fortune. When she held me, was I part of the source of her soul, was I her fortune?

And my brother, Lautaro, he was my hero. When I was a little girl, he was my Moses, who forced me to run toward the star, who held me in the night and fought to keep me with him so together we would win the race with the sky and find the Promised Land. He was like Moses in another way too. He brought me to the Promised Land but his heart couldn't enter, not completely, not ever. Because of him, I was able to be a child even if he couldn't be one himself. Because of him I could breathe and laugh and cry and find the Promised Land, which was a new home with new parents, a new life whole and joyous. Because of him my world made sense and the walls holding my soul together never collapsed.

Tonight when I was lying in bed I remembered something. When we were in the sealing room of the temple, I looked into the mirrors facing each other, the light reflecting back and forth, going on and on forever. But within the mirrors, the continuous reflection of the light changed the color. It wasn't clear, white light like the light in the room, but a soft, transparent bluish-green. Almost the color of the sky. Almost the color of the sea. Perhaps it is the color of eternity. To me it is the color of hope.

When the legendary Greek hero, Theseus, went into the labyrinth to slay the minataur, he took a ball of string, unwinding it as he went so he could find his way out. Every time I look at a star, I will pray that the string tying my brother's life to mine hasn't broken. I will trust that my Thes found his way out of the labyrinth too. I will remember the day our family knelt around the altar of God, who is our source and our fortune.

On March 21, the spring equinox, the day Theseus Lautaro Fletcher would have celebrated his nineteenth birthday, his family went to the ocean, to the rocks where he had fished for the last time.

Rick Fletcher brought his own bamboo fishing pole. It was sunny that day and windy. The wildflowers were in full bloom as they hiked across the bluff toward the rocks where Thes loved to fish. They helped each other traverse the ledge, first Rick, next Meryl, then Dennie, and finally, Blake Taylor. Rick was the first to walk out onto the rock where his son had died. He wedged the bamboo pole into a deep crevasse between two boulders. He would leave it here. He made sure that the words he had carved along the side of it faced the sea: *To Thesesus Lautaro Fletcher, my son. I love you with all my heart.* Then, he turned and walked back to join the others.

Dennie cautiously made her way to the edge of the rock. When her footing was sure, she threw an armload of white petals into the waves. She whispered so no one but the wind and her brother could hear. *For you Thes. Are you asking, 'What is it? Why the flowers, Mina?' God sent manna from the sky. He sent us to angels on earth, a family, our family. We're here. We love you. Maybe he sent an angel to lead you into paradise. Maybe the angel was our mama in Chile.*

After Dennie returned to her parents and uncle, they stood for a moment near the sea, with the wind in their hair. Then, they walked back to the bluffs where Karin and Chris waited with Blake's guitar and a package Dennie had asked them to hold. They sat together on a rock formation. Blake Taylor and Dennie Fletcher's voices rose with the wind as they sang new verses to Blake's song about Moses.

Thes looses the white bird. It rises and turns
Towards sun with its bright flame—we live for it burns.
Waves crash, and we weep as God gathers him home.
Dear Thes, you have left us alone.

As sunset and darkness begin a new day
Alone in earth's wilderness, we kneel to pray
Oh, God of Israel, hear our plea—
Keep Thes safe in heaven with thee.

After the song, Meryl Fletcher read them a poem she had written, a poem to put on the last page of the photo album which celebrated her son's life, a poem titled "Courage in a Gale Wind."

Hawks Tilt
Attempting to soar.
Weathered fences
Climb wind-raped hills
Dividing trees: Fencing some in and
Some out.

The sword of sunlight separates the sea
Into molten silver and raging turquoise.

My son
Dry-eyed, faces the gale.
He stretches his arms to the clouds
And races the sky,
While we walk midst walls of his courage
On earth.

Then, Dennie handed her parents a present wrapped in bright paper and ribbons. Her mother unwrapped the gift and found a journal with an ocean scene on the front. "It's a birthday present," Dennie explained. "Uncle Blake gave me the journal months ago and suggested I write in it. It tells about Thes and me, about our lives in Chile and here. I want you and Dad to have it. From us. From Lautaro and Mina." Meryl Fletcher held the book to her heart. Rick Fletcher hugged his daughter and kissed her hair.

Blake Taylor encircled Dennie and her family in his arms. Then, he gathered Karin and Chris to them. The two families bowed their heads and prayed. As their words reached the heavens, the birds' chatter and the ocean's roar filled the air as a song of life. They thanked Heavenly Father for the young man they loved, the boy who dared to race the sky.

ABOUT THE AUTHOR

As the daughter of a research scientist who traveled extensively, Marcie Anne Jenson learned at a young age that the cohesive strength of friendship spans continents and cultures. She feels deeply that we are all children of the same Heavenly Father winding our way through joys and sorrows in a world that is both broken and beautiful.

As a credentialed teacher and tutor, Marcie has enjoyed working with students of all ages. She has volunteered as a creative writing specialist, an art teacher, and a Support Resource for breast cancer patients. For fun, Marcie camps with her family, explores tide pools, flies kites, and snow skis. She especially loves attending the theater, reading great literature, painting with oils, and, now, writing novels!

Marcie has served in numerous leadership and teaching positions in the Primary, Young Women, and Relief Society organizations. Her publication credits include an article in the *Ensign,* and stories and poetry in *The New Era* and *The Friend*. Marcie lives in northern California with her husband and four children.

AN EXCERPT FROM THE LONG-AWAITED SEQUEL TO
SECRETS OF THE HEART, A NOVEL BY JOANN JOLLEY

PROMISES
of the HEART

PROLOGUE

"You're thinking about him, aren't you?"

Paula Donroe winced as her son's deep voice pulled her back to the present. "Hmm? I suppose," she murmured, setting the bulky Sunbeam® iron on its heel. It teetered for a second at one end of the long, fabric-covered ironing board, then settled into a statue-like stillness.

"Figures," Scott muttered as he slouched against the door frame of his mother's bedroom.

Paula took a deep breath before turning to face her tall, sullen, sixteen-year-old son. *Easy does it,* she silently cautioned herself. *We've all been through an emotional wringer lately, and he's probably hurting just as much as the rest of us. Maybe more . . . he was there when the shot was fired, after all.* An achingly familiar surge of grief rippled through her chest at the thought, and a moment later she felt an empathetic smile rise to her lips. "What do you mean, sweetie?"

"Nuthin'. It's all you ever think about." He stretched out one leg, dug the heel of his sneaker into the carpet, and dragged his foot slowly backward to make a long, wide furrow in the deep pile.

"Well, Scotty," she said, moving close enough to see the sparse patches of adolescent stubble on his chin, "it's only been a few weeks. We all need a little time, don't you think?" She reached out to touch his shoulder and felt the lean, hard muscles tense beneath his over-sized yellow T-shirt.

"Yeah." He set his jaw in a rigid line and stared at the floor.

"You know, honey," she ventured, "if you'd like to talk about it, we could always—"

"Nuthin' to talk about." He shrugged away her hand and smoothed the carpet with a circular motion of his foot. "I gotta go."

Paula sighed. *Maybe next week . . . next month . . . next year.* "Okay. Mind if I ask where you're off to so early on a Saturday morning?" She steeled herself for the all-too-familiar response.

"The clubhouse."

"I see." Her voice was deliberately pleasant, even though she wanted to lash out at him, tell him he should find better things to do with his life than spend every waking moment with that useless gang of his. *But you can't risk driving him even further away,* she reminded herself. *Just love him and be patient—remember the eternal perspective. Let him know you care, and eventually he might return the favor.* "And how are the Crawlers doing these days?"

"Cool."

"That's nice, dear." *Patience—that's the key. Perhaps one day he'll actually speak to you in sentences of more than three words.* "Try to be home at a reasonable hour, will you?"

"Right," he growled, disappearing quickly into the hall. A few seconds later, she heard the front door slam.

Shaking her head, Paula turned back to the ironing board. She carefully smoothed the crinkled front panel of a pale-blue oxford shirt, dampened it with a spray bottle, and lowered the iron to the fabric. A slow hissing sound accompanied a few light bursts of steam as the rumpled cotton cloth yielded to the hot metal and tightened, then relaxed into a polished, wrinkle-free surface.

For some unexplained reason, this simple act of ironing had, over the last month or so, become a comfortable and comforting routine for Paula. She had moved the ironing board upstairs to her bedroom, where she now stood facing the open window overlooking the front yard of her suburban home in Woodland Hills, California. In this peaceful setting, she would sometimes spend hours banishing the wrinkles from a large assortment of shirts, blouses, and slacks. Her favorite was 100% cotton. None of the permanent-press garments would rumple enough to give her the satisfaction of restoring their original crispness. But cotton—there was a fabric she could really work with. Its wrinkles were so deep and defined that by the time she had sprayed and ironed and smoothed and creased, she was in absolute control. Maybe that was it—the sense of control. It was what she needed most in her life at the moment. If she couldn't quite get the wrinkles in her mind and heart straightened out, at least she could take care of the wrinkles in her laundry.

On this Saturday morning in mid-January, Paula now returned to the thoughts that had absorbed her before Scott's interruption. Yes, she'd been thinking about him—about *both* of them. Her mind roamed over the details of her life since that bleak day in early November when her world had changed forever. TJ, her bright, funny, basketball-crazy twelve-year-old son, had been shot in a random act of violence as he and Scott and some friends had cruised the streets of downtown Los Angeles. He had lived less than a day; and in many ways Paula had felt that his senseless death was her fault. They had argued that morning because he wanted to join the Mormon Church. Paula had flatly refused to give her permission, and TJ, in his frustration, had taken off with Scott. Hours later, the final moments of his life had played themselves out in a cold, indifferent hospital room.

But it hasn't been all bad, Paula reminded herself as she nudged the tip of the iron into a v-shaped pleat on the back of the shirt. *There have been miracles, too.* She smiled, relaxing a little as the warmer memories took hold. After TJ's death, the Mormon missionaries, Elders Richland and Stucki, had taught her the gospel, and she had finally come to understand why her young son had been so determined to join the Church: it was *true*. On a golden morning just before Thanksgiving, she and Millie, her housekeeper and friend, had been baptized. TJ had been there, too, dressed in white, a joyful grin illuminating his freckled face. Paula had seen him.

Then had come the greatest miracle of all. "I still can't believe it," Paula whispered softly as she pressed the hot iron against the shirt's collar. For the thousandth time, she relived the heart-stopping moment when she had realized that Elder Mark Richland, the tall, clear-eyed, earnest young missionary who had agonized over TJ's death and moved Paula to tears with his testimony, was her son. Her *son!* Her heart had told her it was true the moment she'd seen a distinctive bumble-bee-shaped birthmark on the inside of his elbow when he removed his suit jacket during Thanksgiving dinner. Twenty-two years earlier, in the wake of the tragic death of her young husband and estrangement from her parents, she had pressed trembling lips to that birthmark just moments before giving up her day-old baby for adoption. Unknown to her, a Mormon family in Idaho had raised him to be an extraordinary young man; and then some divine force beyond any human comprehension had brought him to California and back into Paula's life. "Thank you, Father," she breathed.

As quickly as it had come, her expression of gratitude was submerged in a wave of doubt, even despair. *But where is he now?* she questioned silently. She knew where he was, of course—home on a farm just outside Roberts, Idaho, where he'd been since the first of December, the final day of his mission. They had stood together in the Los Angeles airport saying their good-byes, she knowing the marvelous secret of his parentage, wondering when and how she would ever be able to tell him. Then, placing his lips close to her ear, he had whispered that *he knew.* He had seen the look in her eyes that Thanksgiving Day, had discerned the meaning in her subtle questions about his family, and now confirmed the joyful truth at their moment of parting. When she'd caught her breath, they had embraced, wept, promised to stay in touch. Knowing he was on his way to a long-awaited family reunion, she would stand back and let him make the first contact. "Call . . . write . . . whatever," she had whispered. "Whenever you're ready. I'll be waiting."

"I will," he had promised.

Paula's brow furrowed, and the iron stopped its rhythmic back-and-forth motion. *That was six weeks ago,* she mused. *Christmas, New Year's . . . times I would have expected a call, or at least a card. What's going on?* She plunged deeper into thought, considering all the troubling possibilities. *Is he ill? Has he decided he doesn't want me in his life after all? Has he told his parents, and have they forbidden him to contact me? Do I mean anything at all to him, or am I just another notch on his missionary name tag? Will I ever see or hear—*

"Ow-w-w!" Paula smelled the seared flesh on one side of her finger almost at the same instant she felt the white-hot pain. "Nice move, Donroe," she sputtered as a fiery red welt erupted and spread itself alongside her knuckle. "What were you thinking? That's your problem, you know—you were thinking *too much.*" Her reflexes took over, and she raised the finger to her lips and sucked hard. With her other hand, she yanked on the iron's garish blue cord until the socket gave up and let go. Lifting the iron, she saw an angry brown scorch mark on the shirt's pale-blue sleeve. "So much for being in control," she muttered.

With her throbbing finger still pressed to her lips, she set the iron on its heel and moved a few steps to her bed. Sinking onto the polished-cotton comforter, she began to rock back and forth, her eyes closed tightly in an effort to shut out the pain. *Get a grip, girl,* she chided. *It's only a little burn.* But somehow this minor insult to her flesh was the last straw, and a suffocating wave of grief and helplessness washed over her. Hot tears coursed down her cheeks as she thought of her three sons—TJ, who now lay beneath a mound of cold earth in the Rolling Hills Cemetery; Scott, who seemed to be moving further away from her by the minute; and Mark Richland, the precious child she had found but now seemed to have lost again. "What's it all for, Heavenly Father?" she sobbed. "What's it all for?"

Falling back against the pillows, Paula yielded to the emotion of the moment. She wept until exhaustion stilled her slender body and she fell into a heavy, dreamless sleep.